Discoveries

Brock Archer

Brock Archer Arts   Phoenix

DISCOVERIES

www.brockarcher.net

Author's Note

This book is a work of fiction. Any resemblance to persons or events is strictly coincidental.

An earlier draft of this story, written in 2014 before the Supreme Court decision legalizing same-sex marriage, appeared online as *Southern Decadence*. In this new and revised story, readers familiar with the earlier draft will find substantial modifications in this version, including the addition of a whole new subplot and a completely different ending.

In order to give the novel more credence and believe-ability, the real names of some actual people, places, and products are included in this work of fiction. However, no claim of any relationship between the author and these establishments is made, and they are not responsible or liable for any of the content of this book.

1　　When Darkness Falls

"Shotgun!" yelled Jeremy. "I called it first."

Wade had to laugh at Jeremy's childlike behavior as he loaded the young lovers' luggage into the back of the pickup. Oh, at 25, Jeremy was hardly a child. In fact, since his parents died in that car accident when he was in college, Jeremy—already a young man with a solid head on his shoulders—had matured into a very capable ranch owner and businessman. Still, Wade hadn't seen Jeremy this happy in quite some time.

As Wade drove the pickup down the long dirt driveway, Jeremy alternated between surveying the large ranch that he had inherited and admiring the beautiful young woman sitting between him and Wade. Soon they would be at the airport and then in New Orleans. Life is good, he concluded. *Life is good.*

Jeremy Travis had been quite content to continue "living in sin" with his girlfriend Amy on his 16,000-acre ranch outside of Cheyenne, Wyoming, but after almost a year of shacking up together, she really wanted to get married, and he loved her too much to lose her, so he consented. In fact, he loved her so much that he was even willing to have the wedding on Labor Day in her hometown of New Orleans. Why not? He had no family left, and he had never been to New Orleans. Hell, he had never really been outside of Wyoming—except for a few trips to cattle auctions in Denver with his dad.

So, when Amy suggested that they fly down on the Thursday before Labor Day, he quickly agreed. While she took care of some last-minute details, he would get to enjoy a mini-vacation in the Big Easy.

Though Jeremy was not looking forward to a formal wedding (what man ever is?), he was excited about seeing New Orleans. And enjoying the subsequent honeymoon in the Bahamas, of course. He assumed that he and Amy would both stay in her parents' home in New Orleans' historic Garden District—hell, from all she had said, it was certainly big enough—but Amy had protested that seeing each other so soon before the wedding would be unlucky, so she made arrangements for Jeremy to stay with her brother Ford in his apartment in the French Quarter.

Ford was one of New Orleans' finest, a rookie police officer, and the two men shared a pleasant conversation over the phone about a week before the big event. Ford explained that he would be working the late shift on Thursday but that he could leave the apartment unlocked for Jeremy.

"Oh, don't do that," Jeremy insisted. "I'd really like to take the time to explore the French Quarter. Why don't you give me a ring on my cell phone when you get off duty, and I'll tell you where I am so you can pick me up."

It was early evening when their plane arrived and they were met at the airport by Mr. and Mrs. Leveque, Amy's parents, who took them for a nice, leisurely dinner at Commander's Palace. The Leveques pleaded with Jeremy to stay at their house until Ford got off duty, but Jeremy explained the arrangements that the two young men had made.

"The French Quarter?" protested Mrs. Leveque. "But this is Southern Decadence Weekend!"

Southern Decadence? It sounded intriguing to Jeremy, but he didn't want to sound licentious in front of his new in-laws-to-be, so he asked innocently, "What's that?"

"That's when the ho...the gays...take over the Quarter," cautioned Mrs. Leveque. "It's not a good time for a fine young man such as you to be walking the streets alone at night down there."

"Oh, don't worry, Mother. Jeremy is gorgeous," Amy interceded, squeezing her lover's bulging biceps and smiling adoringly into his crystal blue eyes, "so I wouldn't be surprised if he got hit on—more than once—but he's a big boy; he can take care of himself. Besides, he's mine, and all he has to do is say 'thank you, not available,' and they won't bother him. They're gay, Mother, they're not criminals."

The strain on Mrs. Leveque's face betrayed her desire to protest, but she knew better than to fight with her obstinate daughter—especially on the weekend before her wedding.

The oppressive Louisiana heat and humidity got the better of Jeremy, so when the Leveques dropped him off at the corner of Canal Street and Bourbon Street, he left his coat and tie with Amy and made arrangements to get his luggage in the morning. As her parents left to take Amy home with them, Jeremy unbuttoned his shirt halfway and ventured into the famous Vieux Carré.

Yes, Jeremy Travis was about to enter a very different world. Little did he know just how different it would be.

Jeremy could not have left his sprawling ranch in better hands than those of his foreman, Wade Dawkins. Looking like he had just stepped out of a Bill Gollings painting, Wade was the quintessential cowboy—only better looking than most. He had worked for Jeremy's parents for years and had become a trusted family friend as well as a very dependable employee. Strong, confident, and very capable, the 40-year-old foreman was like an uncle to Jeremy, especially after his parents died. Of course, the situation with Randy did complicate matters, but Jeremy felt very confident that Wade could manage that situation along with everything else.

Randy, Wade's 17-year-old son, was indeed a handful. Wade's wife Cindy had taken Randy with her to Chicago when she walked out several years ago. Cindy was a city girl, and Wade had always been a country boy. No matter how hard he tried, Wade just couldn't do anything right by Cindy. That didn't stop her, though, from dumping Randy on him when the kid got to be too much for her to handle.

Randy had become increasingly rebellious. He had fallen in with the wrong crowd and gotten into drugs. He'd also gotten into trouble so many times at school that the principal finally drew the line in the sand and told Cindy that Randy would not be allowed back at the school in the fall. At her wit's end, she finally shipped the kid back to his father in Wyoming. "Maybe you can straighten him out," she ranted.

Jeremy, realizing that Wade had his hands full and knowing that he would be away for at least a week, had authorized Wade to hire a couple more ranch hands, which he had done at the beginning of the month.

Despite all these extra stresses, when Jeremy got on the plane to New Orleans, he knew that he could focus on his upcoming wedding and not have to worry at all about the ranch.

It had been an unusually busy week for Laramie County Sheriff Nick Scarpelli, and today was no exception. In addition to the usual traffic accidents, domestic violence calls, and assorted petty crimes and misdemeanors, there had been that bank robbery in Cheyenne just that afternoon, and even though that incident fell under the jurisdiction of the city police, his department had been called upon to keep an eye out for the robbers beyond the city limits.

"Damn," mumbled the sheriff at his car radio, which squawked obnoxiously as he pulled into his driveway after an especially long day. *I left St. Louis to get away from shit like this.*

Nick Scarpelli had grown up on the streets of St. Louis. He had been a decent kid, but trouble just seemed to follow him around. Like the time he was out joyriding with some of the neighbor kids when they decided to hold up a liquor store. Though Nick was unaware of their intentions and took no direct part in the robbery, he was arrested along with the others. Fortunately for Nick, his public defender was able to plea bargain for leniency, and Nick was able to avoid a jail term. However, he had to agree to join the Army. "Maybe they can straighten you out," said the judge.

Actually, Nick was glad for the opportunity to make a fresh start, and he responded well to the Army regimen, developing some noticeable leadership qualities which lifted him to the rank of lieutenant. Though he liked the military life, he had discovered that he really could make a decent life for himself, so he spent his spare time completing his G.E.D., and when he left the Army, he signed up for the Army Reserves and then went on to get a degree in criminology from the local campus of the University of Missouri. With his college degree, he joined the St. Louis Police Department and worked his way up to detective captain. After nearly 20 years, the job was starting to get old, but then something dramatic happened. Abuja.

Nick survived "the accident," but it left him with more than a few scars—emotional as well as physical. So much for returning to the police department. No big deal. Nick had had enough of wars, urban ones as well as foreign ones. In rehab, Nick heard another patient telling stories of growing up in Wyoming. That's what I need, thought Nick —some place remote and peaceful.

"No problem," said the Wyoming lad when Nick asked him about getting a job in Wyoming. "I've got connections." And, man, did he ever! His father was no less than the governor of the state. The governor, in fact, offered Nick a position as commandant of the Wyoming Law Enforcement Academy in the town of Douglas, about 125 miles north of Cheyenne. The job involved more administration than criminology, but it seemed like a reasonable alternative to Nick at the time.

Then, politics intervened. A routine audit of the Laramie County Sheriff's Department uncovered "irregularities." It remained to be seen whether someone was stealing money from the public coffers or whether the problem was just shitty management, but either way, the problem seemed to be widespread and was affecting not only the sheriff's office, but the entire political establishment. Just as the scandal was about to boil over, the sheriff suffered a fatal heart attack, and the county commissioners, now in complete disarray, could not agree on a successor to fill the position until the next election. Civic and business leaders pleaded with the governor to intervene.

"It'll just be a temporary assignment," the governor assured Nick when he asked him to take the appointment. "Just for a few weeks until we can arrange a special election." A few weeks, however, soon stretched into several months. What's more, even though the governor had promised Nick that the job would be mostly administrative, the scandal had touched more employees in the department than just the sheriff, and Nick quickly found himself understaffed, which meant that he had to spend far more time in the field than in his temporary office.

The voice squawking and scratching its way out of the black box in Nick's car demanded his attention: "Ambulance sent to Travis Ranch. Possible homicide."

It wasn't long before Jeremy understood why Mrs. Leveque had objected to dropping him off at the French Quarter. He couldn't believe his eyes. Men were dancing in the streets, many of them half naked—or worse—groping and kissing each other in broad daylight. Well, not exactly broad daylight, but since it was Daylight Saving Time and not yet September, there was still enough light to witness the debauchery playing out before him.

Amy was right, too. He did get propositioned more than once. Why not? At 25 years of age and 6'2" he had developed a well-toned, muscular body from working on the ranch, and he was damn good looking to boot. His brownish blond hair hung in a short bang over his forehead, and then, of course, there were those sparking blue eyes that had melted Amy's heart. Even the way he walked commanded attention—self-assured without being arrogant. He had been extremely popular with the girls in high school and college, so why wouldn't gay men find him attractive as well?

With each proposition, he followed Amy's suggestion (or was it an order?) and simply thanked the admirer and proclaimed that he was already spoken for. Still, more than one man who had had too much to drink threw himself at the cowboy and groped his pecs, ass, or crotch. His first instinct was to punch them out, but he remembered what Amy had said: they're gay, they're not criminals. Besides, he had seen plenty of straight guys get a little out of hand at the college beer busts he had attended, and this was really no different.

If he was unprepared for his introduction to Bourbon Street, he was completely shocked with what he saw when he turned and walked a few blocks up St. Ann. There, between two cars across the street, he saw a man down on his knees servicing another man. Then, they switched places, and the "blower" became the "blowee." Instinctively, Jeremy felt disgusted, but for some reason, he could not keep his eyes off of them. He had never seen anything like it before.

When a police officer patrolling the beat walked toward him, he averted his attention, but the cop paused beside him, looked in the direction of Jeremy's prior gaze, spotted the two men in action, grunted, and walked on. Jeremy could not believe that the cop had witnessed the public sex and done nothing to stop it.

When the two men had finished their business, they glanced over at Jeremy and smiled. One winked at him, and the other licked his lips, and then they started to walk toward him. Not wanting to be accosted, Jeremy veered briskly in the opposite direction. He turned at the first corner and quickly ducked into the first bar that he came to. It all happened so fast that he did not notice the nameplate, The Talon, or the rainbow flag flying above the door, but it would not have made any difference; he would not have understood the significance anyway.

Dark clouds loomed heavy over the Travis Ranch when Sheriff Scarpelli pulled up, the ambulance close on his tail. Before he had even turned off the ignition, he saw Wade Dawkins, the foreman, burst out of the barn toward him— toward the ambulance, to be more precise.

"Help him! Help him!" screamed Wade.

"Whoa, sir. Calm down. Tell me what's happened."

Out of breath, Wade simply motioned toward the barn. "Follow me," Scarpelli instructed the EMTs, "but wait outside the barn until I give the all-clear. And *you,*" he directed Wade, "stay put."

With his gun drawn, the sheriff entered the dimly lit barn cautiously. In the far corner, he spotted two bodies lying on the ground in a pool of blood. Scarpelli signaled the two deputies who had arrived just behind him to fan out and search the barn for any other bodies, dead or alive.

Ignoring his earlier warnings, Wade Dawkins rushed past the sheriff and threw himself onto the ground beside one of the two bodies. "He's alive!" he screamed. "Help him!"

"Clear!" shouted one of the deputies. "Clear!" echoed the other.

Sheriff Scarpelli knelt by the body that Wade was now holding. Feeling a pulse, he hollered for the EMTs. By the time they reached the body, the sheriff had checked the pulse of the other man and verified that he was, in fact, dead—not surprising, considering the amount of blood that had spewed from his chest. When the EMTs lifted the one who was still alive onto the gurney, they exposed a knife lying on the ground.

"Do you know this man?" Scarpelli asked Dawson, pointing to the bloody corpse.

"Yes," Wade replied. "He's Carl Pipkins, one of the two ranch hands I hired earlier this month."

"And the other one?" asked Sheriff Scarpelli.

"He...he's..." stammered Wade. "He's my son."

  Strangers in the Night

The Talon Bar in New Orleans' French Quarter was exceptionally dark; so, at first, Jeremy could not really make out what was going on, but he knew from the jostling and the loud chatter that the place was packed. Slowly, his eyes adjusted, and he made his way to the bar, where he sat down and ordered a beer. He usually drank Coors, but he figured that he might as well try the local beer, so at the suggestion of the bartender, he opted for an Abita.

After a few sips of the brew, he swiveled around on the bar stool and saw that the room, like the streets he had just surveyed, was filled with men groping and slobbering all over one another. Suddenly, it hit him that he had sought refuge in a gay bar. He decided to finish his drink and leave, but having groped through the dark to find his way in and been jostled at every turn, he had become disoriented and now found himself not at the exit, but at the back of the very large barroom. He aimed for a faint light, but instead of being an exit, it turned out to be the restroom. There was no door—only a couple of fully exposed toilets and a urinal trough.

OK. I need to take a leak anyway, so I'll just take care of my business and get the hell out of here.

At the urinal, he drew even more attention than he had before: gasps, whistles, and the most vulgar propositions he had ever heard in his life, and he had heard lots of those. Finishing his task, he quickly zipped up and resumed his search for the exit.

On his way out of the restroom, he passed a door that he had not noticed before. *Maybe this is the exit.* He watched another man open the door and go through, so he followed suit, but it was not the exit. It was another room, smaller but just as dark, packed wall to wall with men fondling one another in obscene ways. He started to back away, but several more men crammed in behind him and blocked his retreat. Before he knew it, one man was giving him a lap dance and another was reaching around from behind to unbutton his shirt the rest of the way and massage his solid pecs and ripped abs. Another began licking at his neck, and a third groped his crotch. He tried to scream, but some deep, dark part of him strangely enjoyed the attention and wanted to experience the perverse adventure, and he doubted that his voice would have been heard over the noise anyway.

All of a sudden, his cock was freed from his pants, and a hot, wet mouth swallowed it whole. Jeremy jerked in shock, but his reaction only excited his captors all the more, and they went to work even more feverishly. Soon, he felt even more hands roaming all over his body, and tongues were now licking and sucking each of his nipples. His head told him that he ought to fight his way out of the room and out of the bar—it would not have been the first time he had been in a barroom brawl (but that's another story). However, his dick, now swollen to its full hardness, told him to stay put and enjoy the ride. It did feel damn good. Of course, he had enjoyed blowjobs before, but never like this. Whatever else he might think of gay men, he had to admit that they knew how to suck cock.

He tried to forewarn the man on his knees that he was about to blow, but whether the man didn't hear him or just didn't care, he continued to suck like a Hoover, and in no time at all, Jeremy shot his load down the man's throat. When his benefactor rose up and leaned forward to kiss

Jeremy on the lips, that was more than he could take. He shoved the man aside and charged out of the room like a bull at a rodeo.

Pulling up his pants and underwear as he exited, Jeremy drew more whistles and gropes from other men standing just outside the door. He turned, again hoping to find the exit, but instead, he found himself at the back of the large barroom, bumping against a pool table and ending up at a bench against a long wall.

His eyes again adjusted to the darkness, and he could see men all around him *in flagrante*. Some sat or reclined on the bench, others just leaned against the wall, and a couple even stretched out on the floor. One large man flung himself up on the pool table in front of Jeremy while another lunged on top of him. Dozens of men stood around, some watching quietly, others cheering on the eager participants. To Jeremy, they looked like the rutting animals he had seen on his ranch—thoroughly disgusting, but strangely intriguing at the same time. Just as he had stood mesmerized at the two men between the parked cars, he now could not take his eyes off the two men on the table or those surrounding him.

Consequently, he barely noticed two other young men approaching him or the two men on either side of him sliding over to make room for the newcomers. One squeezed next to Jeremy's right arm and the other to his left. In the crowded room, they pressed their hot bodies against his. Why would two men give up their positions to the other two? Did they have some special influence in this place?

The best Jeremy could tell in the dim light, the two men were both slightly younger than he was, early 20s. They were just as handsome in their own ways as Jeremy, and their tank tops showed off their conspicuous muscles. Obviously, they both worked out.

"Enjoying the show?" asked the one with the dark hair and piercing black walnut eyes. Jeremy just stammered and went back to watching.

"Your first Southern Decadence Weekend?" asked the one with the red hair and green eyes.

"Uh, yeah," Jeremy managed to squeak.

"Whaddya think?"

"Uh, I dunno. I've never seen anything like this before. I really oughta be going, but I can't seem to find the exit."

"Oh, what's your hurry? This place is just warming up. About an hour from now, it'll really be rockin'."

Jeremy's eyes glazed over. He could not imagine how much more decadent the place could become. They didn't call it Southern Decadence for nothing.

"Here, have a drink," said the one with the dark hair, handing Jeremy a bottle of beer. "Name's Brad. This here's Francis, but ever'body calls him Red." Brad stared into Jeremy's eyes, waiting for him to introduce himself.

"Oh, uh...J ..." *Maybe I shouldn't give my real name, just to be on the safe side.* "Jack. I'm Jack."

"Well, hey, Jack. Pleased to meetchya," said Brad, extending his hand. Jeremy (a.k.a. Jack) offered his in return and felt Brad's firm, but friendly, grip. Red's handshake was slightly less firm, but no less friendly.

Brad and Red paused for a few minutes to let Jeremy soak up the spectacle on the pool table.

"Oh, God, man. Fuck!" screamed the man lying on his back on the pool table with his legs up over his assailant's shoulders. A chorus of grunts began to rumble through the crowd and crescendo with each pelvic thrust.

As Jeremy and Brad watched the rest of the show, Red made his way to the bar, and by the time he had returned with another round of beers, the man on top gasped in a fury and collapsed upon the other.

"Now whaddya think of Southern Decadence?" asked Red, grinning from ear to ear.

"I can't believe that people actually do that—not even in private, but especially not in public."

"Well, it must not have bothered you too much," responded Brad. "You could have walked away, or at least turned your head, but you didn't."

"To be honest, all of this goes against everything I have ever believed," Jeremy insisted. I'm strictly a pussy man. Shit, I've never even been in a gay bar in my life." He started to explain that he had only stumbled into the bar to get away from the two men outside, but then he realized that this was more information than he really needed to share.

"Well, we saw you coming out of the Clown Car," said Red. "You must have seen some action in there."

"Clown Car?"

"Yeah, that's what we call that little room—cuz it reminds us of that little car in the circus that's crammed with all those clowns. Hey, I'm not sayin' you're a clown," Red quickly added, seeing the look on Jeremy's face. "Fuck, we all go in there from time to time."

"I take it then that you're both gay."

"Red here's as gay as they come," said Brad. "Me? I just like gittin' my rocks off. I'm like you; I love pussy, but if there's none handy, I'll take it where I can get it."

Suddenly, Jeremy remembered that Brad's arm was still wrapped around his shoulder. He was tempted to run, but he was also still very curious. Besides, from the moment they met, quite a few other men had sized Jeremy up, but Red and Brad had fended them off, so Jeremy felt strangely safe with his new sidekicks.

"So, did ya or didn't ya?" asked Red.

"Did I what?" asked Jeremy.

"Did you see any action in the Clown Car?"

Jeremy stood silent, but the faintest twitch of his lip and the twinkle in his eye gave him away.

"You did! You son of a bitch," chuckled Brad as he patted his new friend on the chest. "OK, come on, out with it. What happened?" The fact that the plea sounded like a teenager begging his best friend for the saucy details of his latest hot date melted Jeremy's defenses.

With a touch of false modesty, Jeremy snickered, "Yeah, I got a blow job." It was part confession and part boast.

"OK, spill," giggled Red. "Details, and don't leave out a single thing."

Jeremy chugged on his second beer and told Brad and Red all the salacious details of his ride in the Clown Car. The two young men poked Jeremy and teased him at key points in the story. When he was finished, Jeremy sighed and smiled, indicating that he had just made a major conquest. As if to congratulate himself, he finished off his beer in one long gulp. The three men enjoyed a nice, long laugh, and for the first time since setting foot in the French Quarter, Jeremy finally began to feel somewhat at ease. So, when Brad suggested that the three of them go over to the bar and have another round, Jeremy agreed.

The three men found only one vacant stool at the bar, so Jeremy sat while Brad and Red each leaned on one of his strong shoulders.

"It's the prostate," explained Red, responding to a question from Jeremy about the exhibit on the pool table. "Just above your rectum, there's a gland called the prostate." Seeing the look on Jeremy's face that proclaimed, "I know what the prostate is, dickhead! Do you think I'm some sort of idiot?" Red quickly added, "OK, I know you know about the prostate, but did you know that it's extra sensitive? The prostate is to a man what the clit is to a woman, and when a dick (or any object for that (matter) rubs up against it, it can bring a man to a climax. That's what happened to Kenny. Oh, that's the guy on the pool table, by the way. Kenny."

"Holy shit! It can really do that?"

"Fuck yeah! Want me to show you?"

Jeremy froze...until Red and Brad broke out in laughter, and then Jeremy followed suit. As if to prove that he was no threat, Red slid away from Jeremy and settled on the other side of Brad, who carried on his small talk with Jeremy.

Brad mostly asked about Jeremy, but Jeremy remained dubious about revealing too much about himself, so mostly he hedged the truth without actually lying. He said that he was from California, which was technically true since he had been born there and moved with his parents to Wyoming when he was only a year old. He said that he was the sales manager in a small company, which was partly true because he did manage a ranch that bought and sold cattle. He said that he was in town on vacation, which was true, at least until the day of the wedding reception. He said that he did not currently have a girlfriend, which he rationalized as the truth by telling himself that Amy was his fiancée, not just his girlfriend. The only actual lie that he told was to give his name as Jack instead of Jeremy.

Red and Brad told Jeremy that they were both natives of New Orleans and had grown up together. Red revealed that he worked as a trainer at a local gym, and Brad, though he seemed reluctant to talk much about himself, identified himself as a student taking courses in criminal justice. "Oh, my future brother-in-law is a New Orleans cop," Jeremy started to blurt out, but he caught himself in time, deciding it might be best to withhold that bit of information. Red said that he and Brad were not really a couple, just "friends with benefits."

"I really should be going," said Jeremy, rising from the stool.

"Ah, don't be a party pooper," said Brad as he lowered Jeremy back down with his strong arm. "The night is still young, and we're just getting to know each other."

By the time Jeremy resettled on the stool, the bartender had produced another round of drinks.

Brad already had one arm firmly wrapped around Jeremy's shoulders, and now, as he engaged Jeremy in conversation about sports and cars, he slowly moved his other hand up and down the man's thigh. Brad paused in the conversation and gazed into Jeremy's eyes...in much the same way that Amy looked at him when she was ready to make love. Jeremy sat transfixed.

Slowly, Brad leaned forward and whispered in Jeremy's ear: "Feels good, doesn't it?" Brad pulled back and watched for Jeremy's response, but Jeremy remained silent and immobilized. Brad again slowly leaned forward as if to whisper in Jeremy's ear, but this time, he gently rubbed his cheek against Jeremy's. His words were replaced by his hot breath against Jeremy's fair skin. He nibbled on Jeremy's ear and then planted butterfly kisses on his cheek, working his way gradually toward his succulent lips. He again pulled back to gauge Jeremy's reaction. The message he read on Jeremy's face was this: *I can't believe I'm letting you do this, but I can't seem to fight it either.* So, Brad gave Jeremy a faint, loving smile, ran his hand slowly through his hair, and gently pulled him close. Their lips met in a soft, warm kiss.

3   Unaccounted For

"I was making my nightly rounds," Wade Dawkins explained to Sheriff Nick Scarpelli at the hospital where the EMTs had taken his son Randy. "I like to check up on things before I go to bed." The whole county knew that Jeremy Travis was away getting married. "He's probably way too busy to call," Wade added, "but if he does, I'd like to be able to assure him that everything's all right." The irony struck him like a knife in the chest.

"Go on," coaxed the sheriff.

"Well, I came out to the barn, and that's when I found them—just like they were when you got there. As soon as I realized that Randy...my son...was alive, I ran back to the house to call for the ambulance. Then, I ran back to the barn and waited until you got there."

"And you didn't touch anything else or move the bodies?"

"No," answered Wade.

"And you didn't see or hear anyone else in or around the barn?"

"No."

"What about earlier?"

"No. After I dropped Jeremy and Amy off at the airport, I came back to the ranch and checked in with the boys down at the bunkhouse to make sure that everything was in order. Then, I came up to the house to write up my daily report for Jeremy."

"And do you normally sleep in the Travis house?"

"No, I have an apartment attached to the bunkhouse, but Jeremy asked me to stay in the house while he's away—just to keep an eye on it."

"And was everyone accounted for when you checked in with the boys in the bunkhouse?"

"Well, now that you mention it, no."

"Oh?"

"Carl Pipkins, the...the man in the barn...he was not there and neither was the other new man, Eddie Culver."

"Did you ask the other boys if they knew where they were?"

"Yeah, sure. They said they hadn't seen them since they went out to the range this morning."

"And your son Randy. Where was he staying?"

"He bunks with the other boys, but he wasn't there tonight either."

"Didn't you think that was strange?"

"Not really." Wade explained how his son had come to live with him and how he had had very little time to try to turn around his delinquent behavior.

Wade's admission of Randy's drug problem came as no great revelation to the sheriff. On his cursory examination of the boy's body, Sheriff Scarpelli had taken note of Randy's pupils, dilated like full moons.

"Look, Sheriff. I know you have your job to do, but I really need to be with my son right now, and I don't know what more I can tell you that I haven't already said."

"All right, but don't go anywhere."

"How is he, doc?" the sheriff asked Dr. Ravi Singh as he exited Randy's hospital room.

"He's strung out on drugs. We'll have to send a blood sample to the lab to find out just what kind. He's got a pretty nasty bump on the head and a number of bruises scattered over the rest of his body, mostly minor."

"No knife wounds?"

"No. All that blood on his clothes wasn't his. It came from somebody else." And the sheriff knew exactly who that somebody else was.

All of a sudden, Randy Dawkins was looking more like a suspect than a victim, and his father Wade couldn't be ruled out either.

Sheriff Scarpelli thanked the doctor and called Adam Holloway, the deputy he had left in charge back at the ranch.

"Nothin'," reported Deputy Holloway. "No new evidence."

"OK," replied the sheriff. "Lock the place down, and we'll take another look in the morning. Call Sheriff Mabry over in Laramie and ask him if he can spare a few men to help out." Sheriff Scarpelli reasoned that Sheriff Mabry probably wouldn't mind since the Travis Ranch stretched over into Albany County, and he had scratched Mabry's back more than once in the few months that he had been Acting Sheriff of Laramie County." (Nick still thought it was odd that the City of Laramie was in Albany County, not Laramie County, which was his own jurisdiction, but he hadn't been there long enough to learn the historical roots of that distinction.)

"Meanwhile, tell the ranch hands that I'll want to speak with them tomorrow as well, and leave a man there to make sure nobody splits. And put out a BOLO on Eddie Culver."

"You want me to call Jeremy Travis?" asked the deputy.

"No, not yet. There's no point in disturbing his wedding. But check with the airlines to make sure that he got on that plane and got off in New Orleans."

From the moment he had set foot in Wyoming, Nick Scarpelli had heard nothing but praise for Jeremy Travis and his people. In the four months that he had been the county's sheriff, he had come to concur with that opinion; on the other hand, he had been a cop much longer than he had been a resident of Wyoming.

Before leaving the hospital, Sheriff Scarpelli turned to the two other deputies who had arrived with the ambulance. With a nod of his head toward the room where Wade Dawson held vigil over his son Randy, the sheriff commanded, "Don't let either of those two out of your sight."

Jeremy could not believe that he had let Brad kiss him. He had found the prospect of a kiss from another man in the Clown Car disgusting, but this was different. Was it because the other man had just sucked him off, or was the difference in the man who kissed him?

Brad again sized Jeremy up, and still seeing no objections, grasped Jeremy's head with both hands and kissed him again, more passionately this time. He gently bit Jeremy's lower lip and drew it between his. He brushed his tongue across Jeremy's teeth and gums. Jeremy began to breathe more heavily, and as he did, Brad stuck his tongue into his mouth and explored every inch of the cavity.

Jeremy remained perplexed at what he was doing, but he actually reciprocated, as he had done so many times with women. He stuck his own tongue into Brad's mouth and swapped saliva fervently. Without realizing what he was doing, he threw his arms around Brad and ran his hands feverishly all over his back, arms, neck and shoulders. He could not get enough.

Jeremy felt terribly confused about letting Brad kiss him, the ordeal in the Clown Car, and the whole goddam fuckin' situation. What the hell was he doing? He did like Brad and Red, though. They both seemed like genuinely nice guys, the kind of guys he would have a beer with back in Cheyenne.

"Well, how do you like it?" Brad asked.

"Like what?"

"The whole thing," replied Brad. "The blow job you got in the Clown Car, the show on the pool table...us?"

After pausing to consider the question, Jeremy answered. "Well, the blow job was fan-fuckin'-tastic! That, I gotta admit. The show on the pool table, I can't believe I actually stood there and watched it, but I just couldn't take my eyes off it."

Jeremy played with his bottle of beer, trying to end the conversation at that point.

Brad again wrapped his arm around Jeremy's shoulder. "And the rest? This? The kiss?"

Breathing heavily, Jeremy continued to stare silently at the bottle of beer. Brad placed his hand under Jeremy's chin and lifted his face toward him. He leaned in to kiss Jeremy again, but just before their lips touched, Jeremy pushed him away. "I'm sorry. I really should be going," said Jeremy rising from his stool.

"No, Jack, wait...please...I'm sorry. I didn't...I won't.... Please, don't go. Please." Was Brad actually feeling a connection with this stranger? Brad had experienced many one-nighters with strangers in bars, but this one seemed different for some reason.

Jeremy paused. Reading the sincerity in Brad's eyes, he reached out with both hands, grasped Brad's shoulders, and lowered him to the stool that he had just vacated. He did not understand why the feel of Brad's hard, muscled shoulders excited him, but it did. He slowly rubbed his hands up and down Brad's thick biceps, again experiencing that inexplicable tingling sensation.

"Look...Brad. I dunno. Like I said, I've never experienced anything like this before. I've never had a man kiss me before. I really don't want to admit it, Brad, but your kiss was different. For some reason that I can't explain, I...well, I...you know...it was...sweet. Very manly, but sweet."

Brad rose up from the stool and, as he had done before, took Jeremy's face in his hands and kissed him again on the lips. Jeremy's resistance surrendered to the warm feeling he got from Brad's romantic kiss and passionate embrace. Smiling tenderly at Jeremy, Brad whispered, "Like many of the finer things in life, sometimes you just have to develop a taste for it, but when you really care for someone, it soothes the palate like the nectar of the gods." *Brad said he was a student. Was he majoring in poetry?*

Brad handed Jeremy his bottle of beer and raised his own, clinking them together. "Well, you ready for another?"

"No, I think I've had enough beer for one night."

"Who's talking about a beer? I was asking if you're ready for another blowjob?"

Jeremy's eyes popped wide.

"Well, you did say that the first one was fan-fuckin'-tastic. What? You got a limit of one a night?"

"No," Jeremy laughed, "I could outlast your puny little pecker any day," he bragged. "It's just, I don't think I want to go back into the Clown Car."

"Well, what about right here?"

"What? No, I don't think so. I'm...I mean...I'm just not the exhibitionist type."

"Oh, just the voyeur type, huh?"

"No! Well, I never thought I was, but I guess I have been tonight. I shouldn't be staring like I have. Shit, man, I shouldn't even be in here, and I shouldn't be getting blow jobs from strange men I've never even met, and I shouldn't...well, I like you, Brad...and you, too, Red. I really do. I wish I didn't have to leave, but I've gotta be meeting somebody."

"Jack, look, it's only 10 o'clock. She can wait a couple more hours for you, can't she?"

"Well, it's not a she, but—"

"Ah, Jack, you sly little devil, you. You really had us believing that we were the first two men in your life, but now the truth comes out."

"Eat me, asshole. You know what I meant."

"I would like nothing better than to eat you," Brad shot back. "And from the looks of that rocket in your pants, I'd say that you're clearly ready to unload another one."

The three men laughed at the verbal jousting.

"Seriously, Jack. My apartment is just a few blocks from here. Walk with me. We'll talk and get to know each other better. If it turns into something more than that, great. If not, then we'll part friends."

"Well, I do have a couple of hours to kill," Jeremy said, looking at his watch. "No strings?"

"No strings!"

"How about you, Red? Are you coming with us?" Jeremy asked.

Red started to accept the offer, but seeing the signal on Brad's face, he quickly excused himself from the affair. "You boys go and have a good time, and don't do anything I wouldn't do."

"Is there anything you won't do?" asked Jeremy.

"Not much," Red grinned.

As Jeremy and Brad walked down Burgundy Street, Jeremy told Brad about the two men he had observed earlier between the parked cars. "Why don't they do something about this?" he asked Brad. "I mean, doing it in the bar is one thing, but doing it right out on the street?"

"Look, New Orleans runs on four things," Brad explained. "The river, jazz, the world's best food, and sex, not necessarily in that order. Without any one of those things, the tourist trade would evaporate, the city's tax revenue would dry up, and the cops wouldn't get paid. There's just as much sex in the open during Mardi Gras, probably more, only it's mostly straight sex.

"When Southern Decadence comes around, the locals know what goes on, and if they don't wanna see it, they just stay away. Besides, the cops here in New Orleans don't have the same attitude toward gays that cops in many other cities have. Hell, there were probably half a dozen off-duty cops in that bar we just came out of."

"If they were off duty, what were they doing there?"

"Same thing you and I were doing there, gettin' their rocks off." Seeing the stunned look on Jeremy's face, Brad added, "That guy gettin' it on the pool table...Kenny? He's a cop. And the dude bangin' his ass is a fireman. Here in New Orleans, nobody really cares as long as you do your job."

Immersed in the conversation, neither Brad nor Jeremy even noticed the two men in ski masks lurking in the dark alleyway until they leaped out at them.

5   Mrs. O'Toole

Ben Carter had been Cheyenne's chief of police about as long as there had been dirt in Laramie County. While most men his age would have retired years earlier, Ben knew that his life would be empty without his work. A burly bear of a man, he cultivated an image of a tough ogre, but anybody who had been in Cheyenne any length of time had come to find that he was really just a great big teddy bear. Still, when it came to crime, he was tough as nails.

Mattie O'Toole was tougher. Folks who knew her liked to say that the octogenarian had tamed the dinosaurs that once roamed the Wyoming hills and plains.

Before Sheriff Nick Scarpelli had gone to the hospital to interview Wade Dawkins, before he had even gotten the call to go out to the Travis Ranch, Police Chief Ben Carter was checking up on Mattie O'Toole at the same hospital.

"Take me home right this minute, Benjamin Carter," she demanded. "I'm perfectly healthy. Didn't need to be dragged in here in the first place."

"Well, you had a bit of an adventure this afternoon, Miss Mattie. We just want to be sure that you're all right."

"Didn't I just tell you I'm perfectly healthy? Now take me home."

"As soon as the doctor gets back. Meanwhile, I'd like to ask you a few questions if you don't mind."

"Oh, all right. I guess that's your job."

"Yes ma'am, it is," Ben suppressed a chuckle. "Now, you were in the bank this afternoon when it was robbed, is that right?"

"You know it is, Ben, or you wouldn't be here."

"Right. Now, about what time was that?"

"It was exactly two twenty-three." Ben raised an eyebrow. "I looked at my watch just to be sure I had enough time. I had an appointment with Loretta at three to get my hair done, and now I'm going to have to reschedule. Poor Loretta's going to think I stood her up."

"I'm sure she's not upset...maybe a little concerned. I'll call and let her know that you're OK."

"Thank you, Ben, but you don't need to do that. I can call her myself."

"Now, Miss Mattie, did you see the men enter the bank?"

"Of course, I did. There were two of them. They were wearing black ski masks and flashing their guns around and cursing up a storm. People have got no manners at all these days."

"No ma'am. So, you can't really identify them?"

"I just told you they were wearing ski masks. Maybe you should have your hearing checked while you're here, Ben."

"I meant that maybe you recognized their voices or something else they might have been wearing."

"Oh, sorry, Ben. No, I can't say that I did."

"What did the men say?"

"They told everybody to lie down on the floor, and I told them they could go to hell."

"Really? And what did they do then?"

"The big one swung his gun in my face, so I hit him with my cane." Ben didn't know whether to gasp or burst out laughing. "He started to take a swing at me, but the other one stopped him...muttered something about his mama, but I didn't quite catch it. He pulled a chair up to the counter and told me I could sit there while they finished their business."

"And then what?"

"Well, they collected the money and skedaddled. When I looked out the window, I saw a white Camry pulling away from the curb. I didn't actually see them get in it, but since that's the only car that was moving at the time, I'd guess they were."

Once Chief Carter had determined that Mattie O'Toole had no more useful information regarding the robbery, he chatted with her about the weather, her garden, and current events until the doctor returned and gave her a clean bill of health. Then, he drove her home and accepted a cup of coffee and a slice of chokecherry pie—homemade, of course—before calling it a day.

"Hand 'em over," demanded one of the masked men on Burgundy Street. "Your wallets, your watches, and any other jewelry you got on you."

Jeremy froze, but Brad shot back, "I don't think so, dude. Now, why don't you step aside, and we'll be on our way."

Clearly not expecting Brad's calm and collected response to the situation, the man, apparently the alpha of the two, whipped out a pocketknife and screamed, "This ain't no nuh-go-shee-ay-shun, DUUUDE! Now, hand it over before I slit your pretty little throats." Following the blade's lead, the other man pulled a pipe out from behind his back.

Brad slowly raised his arm and nudged Jeremy behind him, shielding him from any potential attack. Evidently, he did not realize that Jeremy could take care of himself.

"I really don't wanna see you guys get hurt," said Brad, "so why don't you just put those toys down and back away."

But Brad's words only seemed to irk the attacker all the more. With his arm outstretched, he lunged at Brad with the knife, but Brad quickly dodged the assailant, turned on him, and, slamming his arm across his knee, disarmed him. Instantly, the other masked man sprang at Brad with the pipe, but Jeremy leaped over Brad's back and decked the man. He never saw Jeremy coming. Twisting the alpha thug's arm, Brad threw him up against the wall and, with the man's own belt, tied his hands behind his back. He did the same with the other man, still lying on the pavement.

"Damn, you were good!" exclaimed Jeremy.

"You weren't so bad yourself, Superman."

Jeremy grinned at the compliment. "So, what do we do with them now?"

"We've only gone three blocks from the bar, so let's drag 'em back down there and hand 'em over to Kenny. He's off duty, but he'll take care of it."

"Won't we have to give a statement or something?"

"Yeah, but that can wait until tomorrow. Right now, let's just dump this trash and hightail it over to my apartment. I think we could both use another couple of drinks and a soft, comfortable couch right now."

The encounter had actually made Jeremy feel closer to Brad and less nervous about going over to his apartment.

"Nice place," said Jeremy, looking around Brad's well-decorated apartment.

"Thanks. My sister gets all the credit. I have no eye for beauty...not that kind anyway," said Brad, winking at Jeremy. "Make yourself comfortable. Take your shoes off. Take your shirt off. Take your pants off."

Jeremy chuckled as he sat down on the sofa, knowing that Brad was only half joking. He did kick off his shoes, but that was as far as he went.

"I don't know about you, but I'm ready for something stronger than a beer. How about a scotch?"

"You know, after what we just went through, I could use a scotch right now."

Returning with the drinks, Brad sat down on the coffee table facing Jeremy. Strangely, Jeremy began to feel like a teenager on a first date. As the two men talked, Jeremy gradually relaxed over the sound of Brad's voice—deep and masculine, but also smooth and reassuring. Brad pulled the coffee table closer so that his knees pressed right up against the sofa, and one of Jeremy's knees fit close to his crotch. He slowly rubbed both of Jeremy's thighs. In due course, he removed his tank top, revealing for the first time his hairy, muscular chest. Jeremy had never really thought about men's chests before and whether they were hairy or not, but Brad's really turned him on. The dark coating was not overly thick, but generous, and a treasure trail drew Jeremy's eyes down toward Brad's crotch. *Damn, he's hot! Fuck, why am I feeling this way?* But he was feeling it, and the bulge in his crotch proved it.

Brad leaned over as he had done in the bar and kissed Jeremy tenderly on the lips. Then, he slowly removed Jeremy's shirt and massaged his chest and abs, moaning admiringly as he did. He licked and sucked on Jeremy's nipples, first one and then the other. He raised Jeremy's arms above his head and licked his armpits. An electric shock zipped through Jeremy's body. He had never realized that his armpits were so sensitive before...or maybe it was just Brad. Brad kissed Jeremy again, only more vigorously this time. He burrowed his tongue into Jeremy's mouth, and Jeremy succumbed to the passion. The two men panted like bulldogs in heat.

"I want you, Jeremy. God, I want you so badly."

Jeremy locked eyes with Brad but did not speak. Hearing no objections, Brad kissed and licked his way down Jeremy's torso and rimmed his belly button. Then, he unbuckled Jeremy's belt and pulled off his pants. Jeremy's cock strained to escape his briefs, but Brad did not remove them. Instead, he rubbed his face against them and gently bit Jeremy's dick through the cotton cloth. When he did pull away the elastic band, Jeremy's cock shot out like a rocket.

"Oh, my God, Jack! It's beautiful! It's fuckin' gorgeous! You're gorgeous." Jeremy blushed and laughed off the compliment. "No, really, man. You should be in the

Galleria dell'Accademia right next to Michelangelo's *David*."

"Galleria dell'Accademia?" asked Jeremy.

"Catholic schools," Brad grinned impishly.

Brad stared at the masterpiece before him from all sides and gently stroked it with a single finger, drinking in its beauty. He pressed his face against Jeremy's crotch and took a deep whiff. "Mmm. Smells delicious." Then he brushed the penis with his tongue, just as he had done with his finger, savoring each stroke. He rose up and delicately kissed Jeremy and licked his own lips. Jeremy moaned and Brad smiled.

Returning to Jeremy's crotch, Brad licked around his heavy balls and then took each one in his mouth and rolled it over his tongue. He licked underneath in that sensitive area below the balls, the perineum. He returned to the penis and kissed the head gently before inserting the delicacy into his mouth. It was a lot to swallow, but Brad had had lots of practice, so, with some effort, he was able to stuff the whole shaft into his mouth.

Oh, my God, I can feel his nose in my pubes. Nobody's ever been able to take all of me before, not even the guy in the Clown Car.

Jeremy gripped Brad's head, more for support than anything else. Then, fearing that he might actually hurt him, he let go and gripped the sofa cushion beneath him instead. Brad wasn't ready for Jeremy to cum. He wanted to savor his love stick for as long as he could...hell, he wanted to savor it forever, but there was no holding back. Jeremy's hot juices burst forth like a geyser. "Ahhh... FUCCCKKK!" Brad thanked God that his apartment walls were thick. Jeremy pulled Brad down on top of him, jerking with aftershocks and grappling Brad's body onto his. He wanted to squeeze Brad so tight that their two bodies would merge into one.

After about a minute, Brad spoke, "You gotta let go of me, Jack."

"No, I can't. I won't. I've gotta have you close to me."

"I'm not going anywhere. I'll be here, but you gotta let go of me. You're suffocating me. I can't breathe."

Directly, but despairingly, Jeremy loosened his grip. Shortly, he said, "I want you to stay right here, just like this, forever, but now I'm the one who can't breathe." Rising from the sofa, Brad looked down at his new lover and said confidently, "I have an idea." Extending his hand, he added, "Come with me."

At first, Jeremy struggled to get his land legs, but Brad wrapped Jeremy's arm over his shoulder and led him to his bedroom. As Jeremy sat on the bed and then stretched out, Brad sat beside him and smiled, "Well, how was it, Superman?"

"Oh, God, Brad. I never imagined... I'm...I'm speechless." Taking Brad's hand and rubbing it softly, the way he always rubbed Amy's, he said, "Thank you, Brad. Thank you for helping me to...to...well, thank you."

"I assure you that the pleasure was all mine," replied Brad.

"No, not all of it," protested Jeremy. "Certainly not all of it."

Brad rose from the bed, and the two men just gazed at each other affectionately. Then, Brad slowly removed the rest of his clothes as Jeremy watched. Jeremy had never looked at a man's body so closely before and had certainly never thought of one as being beautiful, but now he did. He actually found himself falling in love with the Cajun god standing before him.

Once he was completely naked, Brad slowly walked around to the other side of the bed and lay down beside Jeremy. He placed one arm across Jeremy's chest and one leg across Jeremy's legs. Jeremy had never lain with a man before, nor had another man's cock pressed against his skin, but it felt heavenly. He so desperately wanted Brad to hold him. He threw his arm across Brad's back and again squeezed him tightly. "Unh!" Then, he rolled Brad over on his back and lay on his side, rubbing his fingers through the sexy hair on his masculine chest, licking his neck, and kissing his face.

He looked down at Brad's stiff cock and admired its size, its shape, and its proportions. He couldn't believe what a fascinating creation it was. Mother Nature really was a genius, and she apparently worked overtime on some people. He was drawn to the sentinel the way some people are drawn to works of art.

He felt compelled to reach out and touch it, though he had never touched another penis before, not even other boys' when he was young. He rubbed his hand very gently over the monument to manhood and caressed the potent balls that produced the seed of life. He marveled at the feel as well as the sight. He had to get a closer look, so he turned and leaned toward it. He breathed in the pungent man-scent and bathed in the erotic aroma. He softly rubbed his cheek against the cock and balls and thrilled at the sensation. He looked up at Brad adoringly and smiled. Then, he slowly turned again to the treasure before him and kissed the golden fruit.

"You don't have to do this, Jack," said Brad. "You don't owe me anything."

"I want to do this, Brad. For both of us."

And Jeremy turned his attention once again to his prize. He slowly licked the dick from every side, thoroughly savoring every slurp. He licked the balls. Never having done this before, he decided not to take the nuts into his mouth because he did not want to hurt his lover. Instead, he returned to the dick and circled the head with his tongue. Then, he opened his mouth wide and slowly slid it over the meat.

He was amazed at how much he liked it: the smell, the feel, the taste. But mostly, he liked it because it was a part of Brad, that most intimate part of this man. He reveled in the thought that he was giving pleasure to a man he loved. No, he couldn't say that. He had just met him. But he was uncontrollably drawn to him. He wanted him, and he wanted to please him.

He slowly took more of the shaft into his mouth and then more. He could not get it all, but that didn't matter. This was his first time, and he would just do the best he could. Mmm...it felt sooo good. Why hadn't he discovered this delight before? Because he had never met Brad before, that's why. Brad was his mentor and his lover. He could suck on this cock all night, but Brad's testosterone had other ideas.

"I'm cummin', Jack. Pull back, Jack. Now, dammit!"

Though still panting from his orgasm, Brad pulled Jeremy toward him and kissed him deeply.

"Damn, Jack! Are you sure you've never done that before? That was sensational."

Jeremy knew that Brad was just trying to be polite, but he enjoyed the flattery nonetheless. *How can this be? I'm actually flattered at being called a cocksucker?* He *was* flattered, not at the suggestion of homosexuality, but at the realization that he had given his lover so much pleasure.

The sex had drained both men. As they lay side by side on the bed, Jeremy wrestled with the idea of coming clean with Brad—telling him who he really was and what he was doing in New Orleans. "You may think this is strange," he began, "but..."

"Don't tell me," Brad interrupted him, "that you're one of those people who does it with gerbils!"

Jeremy wanted to laugh, but he wanted even more to prove to Brad that he could go toe to toe with him in any pissing contest, even a test of ribald wit. "Well, at least it's better than doing it with ferrets," he quipped.

"Depends," Brad shot back.

"On what?" asked Jeremy incredulously.

"On who's on top!"

On that note, Jeremy conceded defeat and cracked up, and Brad followed suit.

After both men regained their composure, Brad spoke: "You were about to tell me how strange you are."

"Hold that thought," replied Jeremy. "All that heavy laughing has 'bout burst my bladder. I'll tell you when I get back from the bathroom."

As Jeremy relieved himself, he mentally rehearsed how he would explain the situation to Brad, but when he returned to the bedroom, he found Brad totally conked out. He gently lay down beside his new lover, but no matter how tired he was, he just could not fall asleep. For one thing, Ford, Amy's brother, would be calling him soon to pick him up, and for another, he had far too many questions boggling his mind. Why had he allowed himself to get drawn into this experience?

Shit, man, what the fuck have I done? What the hell am I doing lying naked with another man in his bed? Why did it feel so good? And then there was the biggest question of all: *How am I ever going to face Amy again? I'm getting married in four days, for chrissakes!*

Jeremy got up and went to the living room to retrieve his cell phone clipped to the pants he had left lying there on the floor. He set it on the nightstand and nuzzled up again next to Brad. He once again fell deep into thought, and Brad remained sound asleep. Eventually, Brad awoke and smiled at Jeremy. "Hi, gorgeous. What a lovely sight to wake up to. I'm glad you're still here."

"Brad, we should talk."

"Hold that thought," said Brad. "Let me go drain my bladder. I'll be right back."

Returning from the bathroom, Brad caught a glimpse of the alarm clock. "Six thirty! Holy crap! I'm in shit up to my eyebrows! Excuse me while I make a phone call." Brad picked up the phone on the nightstand and dialed a number. Two seconds later, Jeremy's cell phone rang. "That's my ride," he announced.

"Hello."

"Jeremy, this is Ford. I am sooo sorry. Where are you?"

"Right here!"

Brad turned and faced Jack. "Jeremy?"

And Jeremy stared at Brad. "Ford?"

"Am I a suspect, Sheriff?" Wade Dawkins demanded to know as soon as Sheriff Nick Scarpelli showed up at the Travis Ranch the next morning. Scarpelli had gone first to the hospital to interview Randy Dawkins, but Dr. Singh informed him that the patient was still too delirious to offer any useful information. Nick also learned that, at the doctor's urging, Wade Dawkins had gone back to the ranch to get some rest.

"Was it really necessary to send your men to follow me home and stand guard all night?" Wade demanded to know.

"At this point in our investigation," the sheriff explained, "I'm not ready to rule out anything, but," he quickly added, "if neither you nor your son killed Carl Pipkins, then we have a potential killer on the loose, and your life could be in danger." True or not, that explanation defused Wade's anger somewhat.

Scarpelli had Wade go through his account of the previous evening's events again just to check for any inconsistencies, though he did not spot any.

"If you'd like, I can have one of my men drive you back to the hospital this morning." Although he knew that Wade's son would still be incoherent, if not unconscious, he really didn't want Wade hanging around while he interviewed the three ranch hands.

Marty Hitchins, Vernon Wooten, and Johnny Duncan were all strapping, ruggedly handsome young bucks in their early twenties, the kind of men who seem more at ease around cows and horses than people. Being more of a city slicker himself, Nick Scarpelli imagined that these cowboys smelled of denim and leather even when they were fresh out of the shower.

While a team of deputies from two counties combed the barn and surrounding area for clues, Sheriff Scarpelli interviewed the three ranch hands one at a time in the main house.

"Yeah, that's Carl's knife," said Johnny. "He carried it with him all the time." Johnny's cute face gave the impression he was much younger than he actually was. Probably got all the candy he wanted when he was a kid, thought the sheriff. The young cowboy's self-assurance bordered on cockiness. "Can I have his knife?" Johnny asked the sheriff. "I mean, he won't be using it anymore, right?" Clearly, Johnny Duncan was not overburdened with humility.

Just the opposite of Johnny, Marty wore a dark countenance that made him seem much older than his years. He was also incredibly withdrawn. Even getting him to say his own name was like pulling teeth. But it didn't strike Nick as shyness. It was more like a defense mechanism. Beneath the shell, Nick detected what, in St. Louis, he would have called street smarts. He didn't know what it was called in Wyoming, but he was sure that Marty had it in spades.

Vernon was the least handsome of the three, but good-looking nonetheless. Confident without being brash; uneducated, but deceptively smart in a worldly, unpretentious way, he came the closest of the three to exhibiting leadership qualities. He was also the most focused—at least as far as the murder investigation was concerned.

Marty and Vern confirmed Johnny's assertion that the knife found next to the body of Carl Pipkins had belonged to the victim himself. In fact, they all told pretty much the same story—except for one extra tidbit from Vern Wooten.

"Last Saturday night," he said, "we all went down to the Conestoga for some beers, 'cept Eddie. He said he wasn't feelin' too good. And Randy, of course. Too young, ya know, and he's never showed no interest in socializin' with the rest of us anyways."

"But Carl Pipkins went?"

"Yessir, he did." He paused. "But here's the thing. After a while, the smoke in the bar started gettin' to me, so I moseyed on out back for some fresh air, and that's when I seen him."

"Carl?"

"Yeah, but he wasn't alone. He was out by the dumpsters talkin' with another fella."

"And did you recognize this fella...this other man?"

"No sir. It was pretty dark."

"Could you make out what they were saying?"

"Nah, they looked like they was havin' some pretty heavy words, but the jukebox was playin' pretty loud inside, so I couldn't really catch what they was sayin'...not that it was really any of my business anyway." Nick Scarpelli had been in Wyoming long enough to understand that minding one's own business was pretty standard etiquette among the ranchers.

Vern paused again as if to collect his thoughts.

"Anything else, Mr. Wooten?"

"Mmm. Don't think so. It probably don't mean nothin' anyhow, but I just thought I'd mention it...ya know...just in case."

"You did the right thing in telling me, Mr. Wooten. You never know when something like this may turn out to be important in an investigation. If you think of anything else, you call me, OK?"

"Sure thing, Sheriff."

One by one, Sheriff Scarpelli re-interviewed Marty Hitchins and Johnny Duncan to see if either of them could corroborate Vern Wooten's story, but to a man, they couldn't...or wouldn't.

After interviewing the wranglers for the second time, Sheriff Scarpelli joined his team of deputies scouring the barn for clues.

"Only thing we've found so far," said Deputy Holloway, handing the sheriff a plastic bag containing pieces of a broken beaded bracelet. "The beads were scattered all over, 'bout four, five yards from where the bodies were."

Hmm. That far, huh? There was something else about the bracelet that didn't quite add up, but Scarpelli couldn't put his finger on it.

"Holy shit! I just slept with my sister's fiancée?"

Jeremy stared back at his future brother-in-law from Ford's bed—shocked, speechless, and stark naked.

"You told me your name was Jack!"

"And you said your name is Brad!"

"It is!" snapped Ford. "Bradford! My folks still call me Ford, but most of my friends call me Brad...JACK!"

Jeremy explained—apologized—that he had used the alias in a naïve attempt at self-protection.

"Actually, that was probably a pretty wise move," conceded the cop. "Better to be safe than sorry."

"Is that why you told me you're a student instead of a cop?"

"Well, I *am* a student. I got into the police academy with an associate's degree, but now I'm working on my bachelor's. Besides, when I meet strangers in a bar, sometimes they freak out if I tell them I'm a cop. They think I'm there to bust 'em."

"OK. I can see that," admitted Jeremy. Then, Jeremy explained the half-truths he had used in introducing himself.

Though he would not admit it, Ford was actually impressed with Jeremy's creativity. He would make a good undercover cop, he thought, and the way the cowboy had performed under pressure with the two muggers outside the bar reinforced his opinion. If nothing else, his sister had chosen a man who would be able to take good care of her. But would he be faithful to her?

"You weren't exactly working the late shift last night, were you?" quizzed Jeremy.

"No, I'm sorry about that, but I figured that with my future brother-in-law staying at my place, last night might be the only chance I'd get to enjoy Southern Decadence this year, so I made up that story. I apologize for lying to you."

It was now Jeremy's turn to be impressed—with Ford's sincerity.

"We really need to talk some more," said Ford, "but right now, I've gotta shower and get down to the station."

The two young men, still reeling from the revelation of their true identities, nearly panicked at the sound of the doorbell. "Who the fuck could that be at this hour? You mind getting that?" asked Ford, marching back toward the bathroom.

Through the peep hole, Jeremy saw a handsome young man holding the bags he had left in the Leveques' car. "Just a minute," he said, quickly retrieving the underwear he had left on the living room floor beside the sofa the night before.

"Hi, I'm Brandon Miller, Ford's cousin, and you must be Mr. Travis. Uncle Pete asked me to bring your things to you. I know it's early, but I thought you might need them. I hope I didn't wake you."

"No, I was awake. Come in. Ford is getting ready for work."

"Where do you want these?"

"Oh, just set them there by the couch. Thanks for bringing them. You're up awfully early yourself."

"Well, when you grow up on a farm in East Texas, you're used to getting up at the crack of dawn."

"I know what you mean. I'm a rancher myself."

"So I've heard, Mr. Travis."

"Oh, please, call me Jeremy. After all, we're gonna be family in a few days." The cowboy offered his hand to the young farmer, whose grip was as firm as his. "I was just about to rustle up some coffee. Want some?"

Brandon smiled at the cowboy jargon. "Sure. I'll see if Ford's got anything to eat. You're probably like me...eat a hearty breakfast before you start the day."

"Yep. I guess that's somethin' all of us country boys have in common," Jeremy chuckled.

Jeremy found the coffee maker on the kitchen counter and the coffee in the cabinet just above it. He pushed aside the fancy foreign imported stuff that Brad had on the shelf and went for the plain ol' American brand instead. Brandon was not so successful. There was hardly any food in the place. "I tell you what," said Brandon. "I know a place just a few blocks from here that serves a terrific breakfast. We can have a cup of coffee here, and then I can take you over there if you'd like."

"Great, but on one condition. My treat."

Brandon tried to object—"after all, you're the guest of honor this week"—but Jeremy insisted.

"Is that coffee I smell?" asked Ford, entering the kitchen with nothing but a towel wrapped around his tapered waist. Before last night, Jeremy would not have looked at Ford's nearly naked, muscular body the way he did, and he would not have noticed Brandon looking at him the same way. Jeremy was still dressed in nothing but his underwear. Had Brandon looked at him that way too?

"Brandon! I didn't realize that was you at the door." Ford placed one hand on Brandon's shoulder and offered the other one in a hearty handshake.

"Yeah, your cousin was kind enough to bring over my luggage," said Jeremy.

"We're getting ready to go out for some breakfast," said Brandon. "Wanna join us?"

"No time. I'll just take some of that coffee with me. Where ya goin' to eat?"

"The FQ," replied Brandon.

"FQ? You know that place?"

"Sure."

"Is there some reason we shouldn't go there?" asked Jeremy, responding to the uncertain look on Brad's face.

"No, it's just that I didn't know that Brandon... never mind. They serve a mean breakfast. Enjoy."

Jeremy wondered about Ford's unfinished sentence and made a note to ask him about it later. What Brad didn't want to tell Jeremy was that the French Quarter Grill, known affectionately to the local gay community as the FQ, was a popular gathering place for gays.

Two pairs of hungry eyes tracked Ford closely as he strutted back into the bedroom to get dressed. By the time Jeremy and Brandon had finished their first cup of coffee, Ford came running out of the bedroom and raced out the door.

"I'm gonna take a quick shower before we head out if you don't mind," Jeremy said to Brandon.

"Of course not."

A few minutes later, Jeremy returned to the living room with water dripping down his sinewy body. Brandon tried not to stare, but when Jeremy lifted his towel to dry his hair, Brandon's jaw nearly hit the floor at the sight of the cowboy's massive tool. *My God, he's not a cowboy; he's a fuckin' horse!* Brandon was hung too, like his cousin, but not like Jeremy. Shivers flew up his spine and across his synapses as he watched the gorgeous stud slip on his tight Wranglers and sexy Justin boots. He hoped he had averted his gaze before Jeremy caught him all agog. All of a

another man for the second time in less than 24 hours. He actually wondered how Brandon's kiss would taste and how his dick would feel in his mouth. The stirrings in his groin assured him that he would not be disappointed.

What the fuck am I thinking? I'm getting married in three days. Already he had gotten a blow job from a total stranger in a gay bar and slept with his fiancée's brother, and now he was ogling Amy and Ford's 18-year-old cousin. *His* 18-year-old future cousin. *His very cute* 18-year-old future cousin. *His fuckin' hot* 18-year-old future cousin. He had to resist the temptation, but it didn't matter. Before he could turn away, Brandon was on top of him. His deep, wet kiss was, indeed, as sweet and passionate as Jeremy had imagined it would be. Yes, he wanted it; he wanted it badly; but he was too stunned and confused to react. Brandon took his unresponsiveness as rejection.

"I'm sorry, Jeremy. I don't know what came over me. I had no right to ..."

"Shut up, you fuckin' sonofabitch." Jeremy grabbed Brandon, pulled him tight, and drilled his tongue into the teenager's mouth. Now it was Brandon's turn to be stunned, but the feeling quickly passed as he joined his future cousin in a tongue-swirling mambo. A couple of minutes later, Brandon withdrew and, in a mock frown, asked, "Did you just call me a fuckin' sonofabitch?"

"Yeah, I did. Why? You wanna do somethin' about it?" Jeremy dared him.

"Yeah. This!" Brandon threw himself back at Jeremy and wrestled him to the floor. Their bodies writhed in uncontrollable passion as they pawed each other madly. Clothes flew in every direction until they were both butt naked.

9   Jurisdictions

Sheriff Scarpelli found Chief Carter's car parked in front of the Conestoga Bar and Grill when he pulled up.

"You apprehended those bank robbers yet?" Scarpelli teased Carter.

"You got your dick dislodged from your ass yet?" Carter retaliated. Nick took the verbal jousting in good spirits. Despite the differences in their ages, Nick Scarpelli and Ben Carter had hit it off pretty well.

Scarpelli briefed the chief on the incidents at the Travis ranch. Of course, the county sheriff was under no obligation to apprise the city police chief of his investigations, but he found that keeping each other informed made for a better working relationship and sometimes led to a useful exchange of information. Besides, criminals didn't always respect legal jurisdictions.

Nick further explained that he was about to interview the Conestoga staff about the mysterious man that Vernon Wooten said he had seen talking with Carl Pipkins. "You're welcome to stick around for that if you'd like," said Scarpelli.

The Conestoga Bar and Grill resembled the set of a 1950s TV western. An old-fashioned butter churn and several antique farm implements adorned the wooden porch that stretched the full length of the building, which was covered with weathered wood slats. A large horseshoe hung over the equally weathered swinging doors that squeaked when disturbed. Though it was midday, the interior remained as dark as a moonless night, the only light escaping from faux kerosene lanterns apportioned around the dark walls. Wagon wheels sawed in half accentuated the wide panel that hung above the knotty pine bar. Spittoons filled with sand served as ash trays atop knotty pine tables surrounded by knotty pine chairs. A juke box, the rare concession to twentieth-century style, balanced the large empty expanse that filled up with tight-jeaned, boot-clad line dancers on adventurous nights. As Nick Scarpelli surveyed the anachronisms, he halfway expected to see Miss Kitty fluffing her petticoats as she descended the sweeping staircase to greet Marshall Dillon at the bar.

Neither the owner nor the employees of the Conestoga provided much useful information to the sheriff and the police chief except to confirm that Carl Pipkins and the other boys from the Travis Ranch had been there the previous Saturday night.

Then, Patty Murano, cute and petite as a prairie dog, whizzed through the bar just like one of the little critters. With auburn hair, green eyes, and a disarming smile, Patty was the Conestoga's most popular waitress, but it wasn't due to her looks alone. She flirted with the boys just enough to get them to keep buying drinks—and leaving big tips—without letting them cross the line. She carried herself with an air that advertised, "Look, but don't touch." Miss Kitty had nothing on Patty Murano, and Nick Scarpelli was intrigued. No, he was smitten.

"Sorry I'm late, Sheriff...Chief. Had to wait for my mom to come over to look after the kids."

"No problem," said Nick.

"Yeah, sure, they were all here. This one," she sneered at the photograph of Carl Pipkins...not much of a tipper."

"Did you notice anything else about him? Anything out of the ordinary?"

"I dunno if it was out of the ordinary or not, but I did see him talking to some guy out back...by the dumpsters."

"Did you recognize the other man?"

"No."

"Patty," asked Chief Carter, "do you think you could draw us a picture of this fella?"

Patty took note of the dubious look on Sheriff Scarpelli's face.

"I may just look like nothing more than a two-bit whiskey slinger, Sheriff, but there's more to Patty Murano than this saloon. I'm only working here to pay my way through college."

"She's majoring in commercial art," added Chief Carter with a smirk, stretching out the syllables of the word *commercial* before accenting the word *art*, which he stopped short of turning into a three-syllable word.

"Looks an awful lot like Ned Beasley," said Chief Carter when Patty had finished her sketch.

"You know him?" asked Nick.

"I don't think anybody really knows Ned Beasley. Pretty much a loner. Even a hermit, you might say. But, yeah, he's got a place down by Harriman. Patty can draw you a map if you'd like," grinned Chief Carter.

Just as Nick was about to retaliate with a gesture of the middle finger, the police chief's cell phone beeped. "Hold that thought," he told Nick, stepping away to take the call. He returned less than a minute later. "We've found the getaway car. It's just off the interstate by Horse Creek Road. I believe that puts it in your jurisdiction, Sheriff." The police chief was correct. The Cheyenne city limits ended at Laughlin Road.

"Well, since you allowed me to interview witnesses in your jurisdiction, I guess I could allow you to investigate an abandoned vehicle in mine."

"Stolen," reported one of the chief's detectives when Carter and Scarpelli arrived on the scene. "We're dusting for prints, but I wouldn't hold my breath. Looks like they wiped it pretty clean."

"If they ditched the getaway car here, they must have had their own car waiting when they got here. Canvass the area," barked the chief. "See if there were any witnesses. And check out any other tire tracks in the area. Let's see if we can find a match."

"Looks like they're headed north," observed the detective.

"Maybe," replied Chief Carter. "Maybe."

"You want me to go with you over to Ned Beasley's place?" the police chief asked as he drove Sheriff Scarpelli back to the Conestoga to pick up his car.

"Thanks, but I need to take care of a few things first."

Instead of getting into his car, though, Nick Scarpelli headed back toward the squeaky swinging doors of the Conestoga.

"She's mighty pretty," called out the police chief as he drove away. "Maybe she'll show you her etchings," he laughed.

"Murano," said Nick quizzically. "You don't look Italian."

"I'm Irish. Murano was my husband's name."

"Was?"

"My husband was a soldier," she replied. "He was killed in Iraq 18 months ago. Never even got to see his son."

"I'm sorry," said Nick.

Finally, Patty broke the tension. "What about you, Sheriff? You married?"

"No," sighed Nick. "I was married, but she—"

After an extended pause when Nick seemed to drift into a trance, he finally snapped back and asked Patty about her family and her college studies.

"I'm afraid I don't see what any of this has to do with your case," said Patty Murano as she poured the sheriff a second cup of coffee.

"Who said it has anything to do with the case?" he smiled very, very tentatively. After another pause that seemed like an eternity, Nick felt a surge of relief when Patty finally smiled back.

10   Ford Returns

Damn, that was the weirdest dream, thought Jeremy, as he rolled over and slowly pried open one eye. *I must have had a lot more to drink than I realized. Five o'clock! Gotta get up and milk the cows.* After draining his bladder and slapping some cold water on his stubbled face, he returned to the bedroom, still too dazed and tired to fully grasp his alien surroundings. He threw back the curtains, expecting to be greeted by the Wyoming pre-dawn haze. Instead, his eyes were assaulted by the fierce rays of the New Orleans summer sun. He recoiled and stared again at the clock on the nightstand.

Five-o-three! Afternoon? No! What is this? Where am I? Lavender walls? What the fuck! My bedroom isn't lavender; it's blue for chrissakes!

The bed, the furniture, the wall hangings—none of it seemed real. Then, he spotted the note tucked halfway under the alarm clock. "Thanks, cowboy. Had to run some errands. Hope you slept well. Can't wait to see you again and pick up where we left off. Brandon."

Brandon? Oh, yeah. The cute kid in my dream.

"We've gotta talk."

The voice startled Jeremy. Reflexively, he dropped the note and turned sharply to find Brad...uh, Ford...standing in the doorway. All of a sudden, it all came flooding back to him. It wasn't a dream. He really did get sucked off in that gay bar, spend the night with his incredibly handsome future brother-in-law (the hunk now glaring at him in the bedroom), and fuck the shit out of the most adorable kid west of the Mississippi.

"And put some damn clothes on!" barked Ford.

Jeremy looked down to confirm that he was, indeed, stark naked. He also realized that he was still sporting a partial boner. Instinctively, he stroked it a couple of times and then looked up again at Ford and blushed. Ford stared back with a mixture of anger and lust.

"They're in the living room," Jeremy mumbled. "My clothes." Ford didn't budge from the doorway. As Jeremy squeezed past him, his half-hard cock brushed against the hairs on the back of Ford's strong hand. He froze. Their eyes locked on each other. Time evaporated. Fire surged in Ford's dark eyes.

"Goddam you, you bastard! Why do you have to be so fuckin' hot?" Ford clamped onto Jeremy's dick with one hand and threw his other arm around his shoulders. He pulled the naked stud close and devoured his tongue. He squeezed his growing manhood and then grabbed his ass to rub their crotches together.

He knew it was wrong. He had come home to tell Jeremy so. It was all one terrible, unfortunate mistake— one they must never speak of and certainly never allow to happen again. *Yeah, right! Tell that to my fuckin' cock!* The battle raged between the dark-haired head on Ford's shoulders and the tingling purple one on his cock, and the one on his shoulders was clearly losing.

Once again, it was the doorbell that broke their concentration. "Damn! That's Kenny. Get dressed!" Ford peeked through the peephole to make sure that the visitor was, in fact, his patrol partner before opening the door. Kenny stepped in just as Jeremy was retrieving his briefs from the living room floor.

"Holy shit, Brad, you're right! He is a fuckin' stud!"

The remark threw Jeremy at first, and then he recalled that Ford's friends called him Brad and that Kenny was the hairy hulk he had seen getting shagged by the fireman on the pool table at the Talon.

Brad (Ford) shot a disapproving leer at Kenny. "Stifle it, man. I'll be right back." He tramped into his bedroom, snatched up a small bag, and began to stuff it with his toiletries and a few articles of clothing. Then, he spotted it: the piece of paper on the floor. He scanned the note from Brandon, dismissed it, and tossed it into the waste basket.

Meanwhile, Jeremy dressed nervously as Kenny stood over him and ogled him like one of the erotic dancers at the Oz, one of New Orleans' most popular gay night clubs.

"Kenny!" scolded Ford. "Let's go!"

Jeremy glimpsed the bag in Ford's hand. "Ford, what's—"

"I'm gonna crash at Kenny's for the rest of the weekend." snapped Ford. "Make yourself at home," he added frostily. "I left a key for you on the nightstand."

"But, Ford—"

Ford was out the door before Jeremy could finish his sentence, and Kenny trailed belatedly behind, grinning as he sized up Jeremy one last time.

11   Randy

Cheyenne's office workers were rushing home to supper by the time Sheriff Nick Scarpelli finished his paperwork and headed back to the hospital where he had left his prime suspect.

"He's awake," reported Dr. Singh, "but he's very weak. Five minutes. No more, please."

Sheriff Scarpelli nodded and walked past his deputy guarding the door as he entered the room.

Seeing Wade Dawkins standing over his son Randy, Nick observed that the boy had definitely inherited his father's handsome genes, but time and circumstances had molded them differently. While Wade Dawkins' muscular body had been toned by hard work on the ranch, Randy's had been forged on the streets of Chicago's south side. Though both men walked with a slight swagger, Wade's expressed reassuring confidence while Randy's betrayed a vigilance rooted in self-preservation. Wade's black hair was cut so short that it didn't seem so dark, but Randy's fell over his eyes like a Gothic veil. Wade's eyes, black as Wyoming coal, floated like pearls on the pond of a Japanese meditation garden while Randy's raged like obsidian stones caught in waterspouts in the River Styx. Wade wore no jewelry except for a watch purchased at a discount store while Randy's ear lobes glittered with strings of zirconium studs.

"Hi, Randy. How ya feelin'?"

The young man glared briefly at the sheriff and turned his head in silence.

The sheriff edged closer to the bed and tried again, gently, but firmly. "Can you tell me what happened last night?"

Silence.

"Look, Randy. I can't help you unless you talk to me."

"Yeah, like you really wanna *help* me."

Nick Scarpelli had seen this attitude before. Hell, he had lived it. Twenty-five years earlier, that could have been him lying in that hospital bed with a cop hovering over him. He decided to try a different tack.

"I brought you something," he said, pulling a plastic bag from his pocket. Randy's eyes widened at the sight of the broken beaded bracelet. "It's yours, isn't it?"

"What happened to it?" asked Randy.

"We found it in the barn." The sheriff took a deep breath. "Believe it or not," he continued, "I do want to help you, but I can't do that unless you tell me what happened. Why don't you start by telling me what you were doing in the barn last night?"

Randy stared at Nick like he wanted to say something but didn't know where to start.

"I know you were taking drugs. What was it? Heroin, crack?"

"Just pot," replied Randy meekly. "I never touch the hard stuff." Nick noticed the eyebrows on Wade's forehead rise ever so slightly, but he decided not to challenge the boy on that point—not yet anyway.

"OK, and did that have anything to do with why you were in the barn?"

"Sometimes I go there to hide out, and sometimes I go there just to crash."

Good. That's a start.

"Was there anybody in the barn when you went in there?"

"No, I don't think so...at least, I didn't see anybody else."

"So, Carl came into the barn after you were already there."

"Carl?"

"Carl Pipkins, one of the new hires." Randy stared quizzically. "The man who was killed."

"Killed? Oh, my God! Carl was killed?"

"You must've seen him, Randy."

"No, I didn't, I swear. I went up into the hayloft to smoke a joint. I crashed, and the next thing I knew, I woke up here in the hospital."

"And you weren't taking anything but pot?"

"No, I swear."

"And you don't remember seeing or hearing Carl Pipkins or anyone else in the barn that night?"

"No! Oh, fuck!" the boy screamed. "You think I killed him, don't you? Holy shit!"

"That's enough!" yelled Dr. Singh, responding to the rapidly increasing tones on the heart monitor.

"Just a couple more questions," said Nick.

"No," snapped the doctor. "Do you want to kill him? Get out! Now!"

Amy! Jeremy hadn't spoken to his fiancée since she and her parents dropped him off at Bourbon Street. *Gotta give her a call.* He needed to hear her voice. Of course, he couldn't tell her what he had done, but somehow he had to pull himself back into reality. He had to make sure that he hadn't completely fucked everything up.

"I know, sweetie. I wish we could talk longer too, but I've got a million things to take care of. You just enjoy yourself, and I'll see you at the rehearsal."

Enjoy myself? That's the fuckin' problem. I'm enjoying myself too damn much, and I just don't understand it.

For the next six hours or so, Jeremy cruised the French Quarter, trying to clear his head, but the din of Southern Decadence made that impossible. Instead of treating himself to a fine meal at Brennan's or Galatoire's, he stuffed his face with hot dogs and pretzels from sidewalk vendors.

When he got back to Ford's apartment, he thought about calling home to see how things were going back at the ranch, but he had complete confidence in Wade Dawkins to manage things. Besides, what was he going to say? "Hey, man, you won't believe who I've been screwing in New Orleans." He tried calling Ford on his cell phone, but there was no answer. He started to leave a message, but he didn't want to sound desperate, so he just hung up. He undressed, got into the big, empty bed, and spent another sleepless night.

12   Topeka, 1983

"Hey, that's *my* sandwich!"

"Correction, kid. It *was* your sandwich. Now it's *mine*."

"But I'm hungry."

"Tough shit," said the older boy.

"What am I s'posed to eat now?"

"You want somethin' to eat?" asked the bully, chomping off a big chunk of the sandwich. "Here. Eat this," he commanded, slapping a big wad of cud on the table in front of the little one.

"I'm gonna tell what you did."

"Well, we'll see about that," said the bully, scooping up the slop and dragging the little one down the hallway to the boys' room. "What the hell are you looking at?" he sniped at the three boys smoking in the corner of the room. Once they had vacated the premises, he shoved the little one into one of the empty toilet stalls. "You're hungry, huh? Eat this, turd," he ordered, stuffing the cud into the little boy's mouth and forcing him to swallow it. As the little boy choked, the older boy added, "Jeez, I'll bet you're thirsty now. Well, here. Have a drink." The little one came up gasping for breath when the bully finally pulled his head from the toilet.

13   Flashes of Light

Daylight clung to its last breath when Sheriff Scarpelli returned to the Travis Ranch. He wanted to check out something Randy had said before driving down to Ned Beasley's place. Most of the deputies who had been scouring the place for clues had left for the day, but one man stood guard over the house while Deputy Adam Holloway guarded the murder scene in the barn. Nick headed first for the bunkhouse.

"I dunno," said Vern Wooten, studying the sketch that Patty Murano had produced. "That could be the man I saw talking with Carl at the Conestoga, but I'm not really sure. Like I said, it was pretty dark." After Nick had left the bunkhouse, he heard Wooten calling after him.

"Uh, 'scuse me, Sheriff. I didn't want to say anything in front of the other boys, but did you say that this man in the picture was from Harriman?"

"That's right."

"Well, I don't know if it means nothin', but I heard the kid...uh, Randy...mention that name a couple of times. Ain't nothing down there. I don't know why he'd ever wanna go there...unless maybe it was to buy drugs or somethin'." Nick thanked Wooten and headed for the barn.

"Sorry, Sheriff," said Deputy Holloway as his boss approached, "but we just haven't found anything out of the ordinary."

"Come stand over here," Nick directed Holloway to the spot where Carl Pipkins' body was found. Then, Nick climbed up the ladder to the hayloft in a spot overlooking the deputy's position. The young deputy eyed his temporary boss skeptically. Nick slowly circled the spot as if looking for some kind of clue.

Holloway dared not ask, "What the hell are you doing?" when Nick lay down in the hay, approximating the position that Randy might have taken when he crashed there the night before. From that angle, Nick spotted a tiny sliver of light reflecting off something at the edge of the loft.

"Toss me your knife," Nick called to Holloway below, and with it, he pried a small object loose from the beam.

"Whadja find?" asked the deputy.

"My guess is that it's the hasp from Randy Dawkins' beaded bracelet," replied Nick. "Brace yourself," he cautioned Holloway before tumbling off the edge of the loft toward him.

The deputy lit up like he had just been struck with an epiphany. "Oh, I get it: the kid waited up there in the loft for the victim, and when he arrived, he jumped him with the knife, catching the hasp of his bracelet on that beam and scattering the beads across the barn floor."

"Maybe," replied the sheriff. "Maybe."

Harriman is a hamlet of about 100 people tucked away in the southwest corner of the county. The town was named for the railroad and banking tycoon Edward H. Harriman, whose Union Pacific Railroad ran through the area on its way from Denver to Cheyenne and whose fortune was used by his widow to foster the incipient eugenics movement in the United States in the early 20th century.

Darkness had fallen over Ned Beasley's place on the outskirts of the town when Sheriff Scarpelli arrived. Not knowing quite what to expect, he decided to leave his car up the road and approach the house on foot. A faint strip of light seeped under the garage door while two male voices echoed off the walls behind it.

Reflections of Abuja flashed across Nick Scarpelli's mind as the blinding light exploded before him and catapulted him backward. It was the last thing he remembered before the lights went out.

14   Partners

On Saturday morning, Jeremy called the Leveque house
to speak with Amy, but Mrs. Leveque informed him that
she had gone out to take care of some arrangements.
"Have you been to Audubon Park yet? It's a marvelous
place, and it's such a lovely day for it." He asked to speak
to Brandon, thinking he might like to tour the park with
him. "Oh, I'm sorry, he had to go back to Texas."

"Is there a problem?"

"Oh, no. Just something he had to take care of at the
farm. I'm sure you know how that is. He'll be back in time
for the wedding, though."

So, Jeremy spent the day at Audubon Park—alone.

When he got back to the apartment, he heard noises
coming from the bedroom. "Ford?" He was eager to see
him again. They really did need to sit down and talk. But it
wasn't Ford.

"Kenny, what are you doing here, and who's this?"

"Oh, hey, Jeremy. This is my partner, Kyle."

"I thought Ford was your partner."

"Other kind of partner," said Kenny, with a wink.

Then it hit him: Kyle was the fireman he had seen
banging Kenny on the pool table at the Talon on Thursday
night. Another piece of the puzzle fell into place.

Kyle was a mountain of a man, the Paul Bunyan type,
built like a brick shithouse. A neatly trimmed beard and
mustache framed his carved face, just made for Mt.

Rushmore. A profusion of fur transgressed the neckline of the skin-tight T-shirt that gripped his massive chest. More dark hair poked out from under his New Orleans Saints cap. His powerful handshake emulated a motorized vice carefully calculated to apply just the right amount of pressure. His physical presence contrasted ironically with his radiant, almost child-like smile. Jeremy understood immediately why Kenny had fallen under Kyle's magical spell. Hell, who wouldn't?

"I said, Brad asked us to pick up a few of his things," Kenny repeated, breaking Jeremy's fixation on Kyle, the gentle giant.

"Oh...uh...why didn't he come get them himself?"

"I think you know the answer to that question, Jeremy."

"No, I don't, Kenny. In fact, I don't know much of anything anymore," Jeremy vented.

Kenny approached Jeremy and placed a reassuring hand on his shoulder. "Look, Jeremy, this is really none of my business, but I think Brad likes you—I mean, really likes you—but you're about to marry his fuckin' sister, for chrissakes!"

"But I just wanna see him, talk to him, and—"

"And what, Jeremy? What the hell do you expect him to do?"

"I dunno, I just .... I don't know, dammit!" Jeremy threw himself face down across the bed and choked back his emotions. Kenny and Kyle glanced at each other and then sat on either side of him. Their warm, comforting hands on his arms and back electrified his entire body, but especially the nerve center located in his groin.

Jeremy rolled over to face the two hunks. "Look, guys. I'm not gay." *Yeah, right! You've just got a snake crawling around in your jeans.* "I don't know what came over me with Ford and Brandon, but I—"

"What? Brandon too?"

Oh, my God! Jeremy suddenly realized his slip. "Please don't tell Ford—or Amy!—it was just an accident. I never meant—"

"Look, Jeremy," said Kenny, petting the cowboy's heaving chest, "what you do is your business. Don't ask, don't tell. Ya know what I mean? But I think you need to decide what you really want. Your words say one thing, but this...." He squeezed the thick hose swelling between Jeremy's legs. "This tells a whole 'nutha story, buddy."

Jeremy lay silent, caught in the dilemma. He stared at Kenny and then at Kyle, who, at that point, was now rubbing his hand along the inside of Jeremy's thigh and against his scrotum. Kenny leaned ever so slowly toward Jeremy and, seeing the desire in his eyes, kissed him. Jeremy transformed from a passive subject to an aggressive participant. When Kenny finally pulled back, Kyle moved in, but halfway into his cautious descent, Jeremy threw his hands around Kyle's thick neck and yanked him tight, blasting his way into the fireman's eager mouth. Kenny lustfully watched the cowboy swallow his lover's tongue and then joined them in a kiss-and-lick slobberfest.

Kyle reached up under Jeremy's shirt to massage his rock-hard chest and ripped abs while Kenny slipped his hand beneath Jeremy's jeans to play with his rambunctious reptile. Jeremy reciprocated, pawing at the two men's hefty baskets. Kyle pulled off Jeremy's shirt and went to work on his nipples, alternately sucking and pinching them. As Jeremy moaned in delirium, Kenny hastily removed the rest of his clothes. Kyle and Kenny worked on their subject from both sides. Each sucked a nip while Kenny rubbed Jeremy's balls and Kyle pumped his shaft. The stimulation was almost more than Jeremy could bear.

But that was nothing compared to what Jeremy was about to experience. When Kenny licked his balls and the tender zone below them and Kyle swallowed his tingling cock, Jeremy nearly bolted off the bed. His screams rivaled the noises of the Southern Decadence partygoers on the streets below. On any other weekend, the neighbors might have called the cops. How could they know that there was already one there?

When the three dicks finally went limp, Kenny rolled over beside Jeremy, and Kyle plopped down on the other side, but first, he retrieved the bottle of lube he had tossed onto the bed and greased his resurrecting tool one more time. Then, breathing heavily and intimately into Jeremy's face, he asked, "So, Jeremy, has that sweet ass of yours ever been fucked by a man before?"

"Mornin', soldier," said Police Chief Ben Carter as he rose from his chair in the corner of Nick Scarpelli's hospital room. "You gave us all a bit of a scare there."

"Wha...what happened?" asked Nick.

"Well, simply put, Ned Beasley blew himself up and nearly took you with him. I spoke to the fire chief, and he suspects it was a meth lab explosion, though it'll take several days to sift through all the evidence."

Meth lab, huh? Nick suddenly recalled what Vern Wooten had said at the Travis Ranch about Randy Dawkins going to Harriman to buy drugs.

"I heard voices," mumbled Nick.

"I'll bet you did," snickered Ben.

"No. At the house. I heard two voices coming from the garage. Two men. And there were two cars parked at the side of the garage."

"Hmmm. I'll tell the fire chief. Fact is, the place was blown to smithereens. Hard to tell just how many people were in that house or how many cars were there."

"Damn! I wish I'd gotten the license numbers of those cars."

"It's a good thing you didn't," remarked Chief Carter. "If you'd been close enough to those cars to get the license numbers, you'd have been blown to kingdom come along with them."

"There's something else you're not telling me, Ben," Nick noted.

"Why would you say that?" asked the older man.

"You're fluffing my pillow," Nick replied. "You're not doing that to make me comfortable. You're doing it 'cause you're *un*comfortable."

"During the night," Ben ventured slowly, "you kept muttering a word."

"What word?"

"I'm not really sure, but it sounded something like 'boocha'."

In a flash, Nick found himself back in time. In Abuja.

The shower was running full blast when Nick rushed into the warmly decorated room in the Transcorp Hilton Abuja. The walls were clad in a sand-colored, richly textured paper with brown and green borders. Three Yoruba prints hung over the bed, which was crawling with lions, tigers, giraffes, and zebras on a quilted tundra. Matching drapes and valences flanked the windows.

"Hurry up, Sweetheart," Nick called to the bathroom. "We don't want to be late for the reception." He knew full well, though, that they would be late. Leanne was never on time. It wasn't like she needed to arrive late to draw attention; she turned heads no matter where she went or what time she arrived.

They had met two years earlier at the veterinary clinic. Nick loved animals, but with his work schedule, he didn't feel that it would be right to have a pet of his own. When a neighbor asked him to take care of her Lhasa apso while she went away for a few days, he welcomed the opportunity. When the dog wouldn't eat, Nick got concerned and decided to take him to a vet.

After signing in with the receptionist, Nick sat in the waiting room with the fur-angel in his lap when in marched a Great Dane with his hulking master in tow.

Sitting next to Nick, the giant ape stared at the mop in Nick's lap and asked condescendingly, "What's that?"

"He's a Lhasa apso," replied Nick.

"You'd never catch me with one of those sissy dogs," sneered the simian.

"Well, some of us are secure enough in our masculinity that we don't worry about such things," responded Nick.

"Mr. Scarpelli, the doctor will see you now," announced the assistant while the ape tried to figure out whether or not he had just been insulted. "Second room on the left."

Entering the room, Nick thought he had made a mistake. "Oh, I'm sorry," he said to the gorgeous woman standing beside the examining table. "I thought I was supposed to bring my dog in here."

"Mr. Scarpelli?" the woman asked as Nick turned to leave. "I'm Dr. Castle."

"You're the vet?" asked Nick in disbelief. She nodded. "Jeez," pronounced Nick, "I'm gonna have to adopt every sick animal in the pound."

Dr. Castle was not very impressed. She had heard just about every come-on there was, but to Nick, it was not just a come-on. He was genuinely taken.

"What seems to be the problem here?" she asked.

"Problem?" asked Nick, his eyes locked on the Athenian goddess.

"The dog," she said.

"Huh? Oh, the dog," said Nick, snapping out of his trance. "He won't eat. His owner went away for a few days and left me to pet sit."

"Well, it's not unusual for pets to fast when their masters are away, but we'll take a look just to rule out any medical problems."

"It's very nice of you to pet sit for your friend," she said, trying to fill the silence.

"Oh, yeah," he stammered. "I love animals. They're great." Normally very eloquent and suave, Nick could not help tripping over his own tongue. He had not felt so inadequate since he was 11 years old.

Dr. Castle checked the dog's temperature, weight, eyes, ears, and mouth, and felt his small body before proclaiming him to be in perfect health.

"But he won't eat," insisted Nick. "What should I do?"

"What have you been feeding him?"

"Just regular dry dog food from the supermarket."

"That's not good."

"Well, he usually likes it."

"He may like it, but it's not good for him. Most dog foods contain ethoxiquin and assorted by-products, which can cause all kinds of problems for dogs. Get yourself a copy of a book called *Food Pets Die For* by Ann Martin and start reading the labels on the foods you buy. Avoid anything with ethoxiquin and by-products."

"OK, but if I buy other dog food, will he eat?" asked Nick.

"He'll eat when he gets hungry enough," she counseled. "I'd give him another day or two. If he's not eating by then, you might try mixing a little canned food with the dry food."

Not only is she gorgeous, but she really seems to know her stuff. He was impressed.

On his way out, Nick bumped into the gorilla with the Great Dane—literally bumped into him. Apologizing profusely—as much in self-defense as anything else—Nick maneuvered past the hulking man and snapped up a business card from the registration counter on his way out.

"Leanne Castle, DVM." Nick kissed the card, slipped it into his shirt pocket, and patted it like a winning lottery ticket. With his movie star looks and natural charm, he had never had any trouble attracting women. The fact that this one didn't fall immediately into his lap made him all the more determined to win her over.

One year later, Leanne Castle, DVM, became Mrs. Nick Scarpelli.

Leanne maintained her veterinary practice after she married Nick. It helped her keep her mind off of worrying about him while he was out on patrol in the streets of St. Louis. Her work earned her a growing international reputation and an invitation to join a scientific delegation to explore Nigeria's Yankari National Park, the best natural animal preserve in West Africa.

Nigeria, situated just north of the equator on the Gulf of Guinea, is Africa's most populous country. More than 250 languages are spoken by as many ethnic groups. The northern part of the country is predominantly Muslim (50%) while the south is mostly Christian (40%). In an effort to unite the country's disparate factions, the government, in 1991, moved the capital from the coastal city of Lagos to the inland city of Abuja.

Having had his fill of traveling in the military, Nick balked at accompanying Leanne on the trip, but she applied her natural charm and convinced him to change his mind. What she didn't tell Nick was that she had a secret to reveal, and she thought that a romantic getaway would provide the ideal opportunity.

Nick removed his jacket and threw it across the king-sized bed in their hotel room in Abuja. He was unbuttoning his shirt when Leanne walked out of the bathroom wrapped only in a towel. "Oh, good," said Nick. "I need to get in there and clean up before we head for the reception." Reaching out to him and running her fingers across his shoulders and upper arms, Leanne spoke seductively, "I thought we might *talk*"—she placed special emphasis on that word—"for a few minutes before we go."

Resisting the temptation, Nick replied, "Sounds great, Honey. Let's do that tonight after the reception."

Not one to give up easily, Leanne lowered her towel, revealing firm, succulent breasts that accentuated her perfectly curved body. "But I have some news to share with you."

Choking back his natural male instincts, Nick stammered, "How about we talk about it on the way to the Ambassador's house?" Torn between the Temptation of Eve and his business drive, Nick walked toward the shower.

"Oh, Nick," drawled Leanne.

"Yes?" asked Nick, turning around to find Leanne standing before him with the towel now covering only her toes. His eyes scanned her form from neck to ankles. Involuntarily, he licked his lips, took a deep breath, and regressed to the 11-year-old boy that he had become when he first met her. Suddenly, his pants and underwear began to feel much too tight.

He stood, frozen in place, as Leanne strolled slowly toward him. Her fingers now tickled the hairs on his broad chest, around his sternum, and down to his navel. She reached down to relieve the pressure at his groin, but it only grew stronger. She drew closer, pressing her soft, enticing breasts against his muscular pecs. She leaned forward and nibbled his earlobe, whispering like a vixen, "Don't you want to talk? I'll make it worth your while."

Drawing one more deep breath, Nick quickly tore off his clothes, brushed his jacket off the bed, and threw himself on top of his Delilah. He thrust his tongue into her mouth, exploring every nook and cranny. He ran his tongue down her neck to her breasts. He licked and sucked each one softly, then vigorously, and then pressed them together and sucked both nipples in tandem. Sensing that Leanne was almost ready for him to enter her, he released her breasts and slid his body lower, licking a path from the center of her chest, around her navel, and down to her soft, furry nest. His tongue went wild—as did his lover.

"Now," screamed Leanne. "Take me now."

As Nick pushed himself up, Leanne reached out to grab his flexing triceps and pull him closer. He lay on top of her and pressed himself into her waiting grasp, slowly at first, and then harder, faster. She screamed. He panted. Their hearts pounded. They both pumped and flinched like wild animals, savage beasts. Their passion rose to a fever pitch. Leanne screamed louder, again, and again, as she released all her tension. Seconds later, Nick exploded inside her— once, twice, and then several more times. He let out a protracted sigh and collapsed on top of her, their hearts beating in syncopation. Shortly, he rolled over, and they lay beside each other, waiting for their breathing to return to normal.

"Oh, I almost forgot," Nick finally broke the silence. "You said you had something to tell me?"

"Yes," she teased.

Rolling onto his side to face her, he asked, "Well, what is it?"

She paused, not knowing quite how to say it, finally deciding that the direct approach was the best. "I'm pregnant."

Silence.

"I know we said that we were going to wait until we had been married five years, and it's only been three, but it just happened. I mean, I didn't plan it or anything. It just happened."

Silence.

"You're upset," she concluded.

"No, no, no," he reassured her. "It's great! I'm just stunned," he said. "I'm...."

He rolled over again, stared blindly at the ceiling, and continued slowly, as a smile crept across his lips, "I'm...I'm going to be a daddy!"

Leanne threw herself at him and planted kisses all over his face.

They talked about when she was due, whether it was a boy or a girl, the need to convert the guest room into a nursery, preparing for college....

"We really should get ready for the reception now," Leanne finally cautioned.

"Yeah, we should," concurred Nick. "The limo's waiting."

He gazed into her sensuous eyes. "We really should go," his voice trailed off. He drew closer to her. His lips met hers, kissing her tenderly. For the second time that evening, they made love, but this time it was less animalistic, more spiritual.

"There you are!" gasped Dr. Jacob Eisen, the head of the scientific expedition, pacing frantically under the portico of the American ambassador's residence. "I was afraid you weren't coming."

"Sorry," said Nick. "We got delayed." Seeing Leanne with her long blonde hair flowing down the back of her sleeveless black evening gown, Jacob guessed immediately what had caused the delay, but he refrained from commenting.

Jacob had made arrangements through the U. S. State Department to launch the collaboration with the Nigerian government by getting the American ambassador to host a reception at his residence.

Upon entering the ballroom, Leanne was drawn immediately to a large painting on the far wall. As she,

Nick, and Jacob crossed the room, Leanne asked, "What is it?"

"I dunno," said Jacob, "but it's certainly colorful."

"It's an Ogubike," said Nick, surprising both his wife and Dr. Eisen.

"Very good, Mr. Scarpelli," said Ambassador Josiah Washburn, approaching from the side. "I see you are a connoisseur of beauty."

Judging from the way the ambassador was eyeing Leanne, Nick wasn't sure whether he was referring to the painting or to his wife. "I'm not an art expert," said Nick, clearing his throat (as if to send a message), "but I do admire Mr. Ogubike's work. Moyo Ogubike is a Nigerian-born American artist now living in Denver," said Nick, addressing Leanne rather than the ambassador. "I saw an exhibit of his work at the Denver Museum of Art when I was there for a law enforcement conference."

"It's magnificent," intoned Leanne, analyzing the woven images of people, plants, animals, and birds. "It's so full of life. And the technique: it's like a cross between a Picasso painting, a Chagall window, and a Gees Bend quilt."

Normally Nick did not mind these business soirees. Tonight, though, he couldn't wait to get back to the hotel to pick up where he and Leanne had left off. Finally, just after midnight, he was able to thank his hosts and drag Leanne away from the "friendly" ambassador.

"Oh, Honey, I forgot my bag," said Leanne as they stepped under the portico and onto the circular driveway at the front of the house.

"I'll get it," said Nick, not really wanting Leanne to go back into the house.

"No, no," she insisted. "You get the limo. I'll be right back."

There were so many limos parked to the side of the main gate, Nick couldn't be sure which one was his. Finally, he recognized the driver and signaled for him to pull up. As the car advanced, Nick walked forward to meet it, but he stopped for a moment and turned to see if Leanne was coming.

Suddenly, he was blinded by a flashing light. At the same time that he heard the deafening explosion, a blast of hot air swept him off the ground and hurled him into the oncoming limo. His limp body smashed like a rag doll against the car and bounced backward onto the pavement. Everything went black. A shred of canvas from the Ogubike painting drifted through the air and landed on his face. It was an image—half an image really—of a dove.

Five days later Nick regained consciousness at the Craig Hospital in Englewood, Colorado. The State Department had transported him there because Craig was regarded as one of the best rehab facilities in the country. The physician informed Nick that Islamic zealots supported by Osama bin Laden's Al Qaeda organization had sneaked into the ambassador's house as part of the catering crew and had simultaneously set off bombs near the kitchen stove and the furnace to maximize the destruction. Leanne, Jacob, the ambassador, and 17 others were killed in the blast.

What the doctor did not tell Nick, but what he would soon learn, was that he would have to spend the next 12 months in the hospital enduring surgery after surgery as well as extensive therapy and counseling.

"Oh, one more thing before I let you rest," said the doctor. "The paramedics found this next to your body when they picked you up." He handed the small, shiny object to Nick. It was Leanne's handbag.

16　Flowers

"Abuja," mumbled Nick, realizing that the hospital room in which he now found himself was not the one in Denver, but the one in Cheyenne. "The word is 'Abuja'," he repeated to Ben Carter's perplexed expression. "I'll tell you about it after I get out of here."

"You brought me flowers?" Nick asked incredulously as he spotted the bouquet across the room.

"Do I look like the kind of guy who would give another man flowers?" snorted the police chief in his gruff voice. "No, these are from your secret admirer. There's a card. Can you read it, or do you want me to read it to you?"

Nick took the card offered to him, but the writing was all a blur. "They're from Patty," said Carter. "The whole town's talking about what happened, so I guess she must've heard about it. She called the hospital, but when she couldn't get any information from them, she called me. Wanted to know if you were all right. I told her you were just looking for an excuse to go back to your cushy desk job at the police academy."

"Whoa! Where do you think you're going?" asked Dr. Singh, entering the room as Nick began throwing off his covers and reaching for his clothes.

"Got work to do, Doc. Got bad guys to catch, ya know."

"From what I hear," replied the doctor, "the bad guys in this case are nowhere to be caught."

"There's still an investigation to be done, and there are other crimes to solve."

"Well, the good news is that the MRI did not reveal any concussion, but I'd still like to keep you here a couple of days for observation."

"I'm fine, Doc. Really."

"I can't physically keep you here against your will, but I can note on your chart that you left the hospital AMA, against medical advice."

"Duly noted," replied Nick.

"Don't worry, Doc," Ben Carter spoke up. "I'll keep an eye on him."

"Oh, Doc. One more thing," said Nick as the physician turned to exit the room. "You said there were bruises on Randy Dawkins' body."

"Yes."

"Would they be consistent with a fall from…oh, say eight feet?"

"Yes, I would say that such a fall could cause the kind of bruises I found on his body."

As he got dressed, Nick filled the police chief in on his findings at the barn and his theory about Randy Dawkins jumping Carl Pipkins from the hayloft.

"Can you take me to the morgue?" asked Nick as Ben wheeled him out to his car. "I'd like to ask the coroner a few questions about Carl Pipkins."

"Of course, I could take you there," replied Ben, "but I won't. It's late, and you need to get some rest. If you won't do it in the hospital, I intend to make sure you do it at home. Whatever you have to ask the coroner can wait until tomorrow."

As Ben drove Nick home, Nick's pager went off. He read the text message, smiled, and keyed in his response. The exchange continued until the two men reached their destination. When Nick finally put away his phone, he was beaming.

"A break in the case?" asked Ben.

"Nope."

"Somethin' personal?"

"Yep."

After a long pause, Nick finally added, "Ya know, Ben, there's really no point in bothering the coroner over the holiday weekend. We can put that off until Tuesday."

"Tuesday? Not tomorrow?"

"Why, Chief. You should know that tomorrow's Sunday, the Lord's day."

"Funny, I never figured you for the church-goin' type, Nick."

"Neither did I, Ben, but then again, I never had anybody ask me before."

17   Best Man

"You're a helluva man," Jeremy responded to Kyle's suggestion, "but everything's been moving way too fast for me. I don't think I'm ready to take it up the ass just yet."

"OK, sport, but just remember where to come when you are ready."

Jeremy smiled back at the giant teddy bear. At the same time, he recalled the advice that Kenny had given him earlier: "You need to decide what you really want." In having sex with Brandon and then with Kenny and Kyle, was Jeremy simply spreading his wings, exploring his new-found sexual interests, or was he trying to escape the feelings he had begun to develop for Brad?

"We gotta be going anyway," said Kenny. "Brad's gonna be wondering why we aren't back with his things."

As Kenny and Kyle got dressed, Jeremy called out, "Hold on. I'm going with you."

"I'm not so sure that's such a good idea, Jeremy," said Kenny.

"I don't care. I've got to talk to Ford, and there's no time like the present."

Reluctantly, Kenny and Kyle acquiesced.

When the three men got to Kenny and Kyle's apartment, they heard primal moans and screams emanating from the guest room. "Sounds like Brad's entertaining right now. We'd better just wait 'til he comes out."

Kyle mixed some drinks while Jeremy blazed a footpath in the living room carpet. Nearly an hour later, a very attractive young woman exited the back of the apartment, buttoning up her blouse as she headed for the door. A few minutes later, Red, the physical trainer Jeremy had met at the bar with Brad, emerged, zipping up his denim shorts. Directly behind him came Brad, clad in nothing but his police cap and gun belt. *Daammnn sexy.*

"Jeremy, what the fuck are you doing here? Never mind. I don't need to know. Just don't let the door hit you on your way out."

"Wait, Brad," said Kenny, blocking him from returning to the bedroom from which he had just come. "Hear him out. I don't know what he intends to say, but I do know that the two of you have got to work this thing out."

Reluctantly, Brad agreed.

"And put some damn clothes on!" Jeremy mocked.

Hearing his own words thrown back at him brought a defenseless smile to Brad's lips. He went to the bedroom, put on a comfortable warm-up suit, and returned to the living room.

"We should leave the two of you alone," said Red.

"Wait. Before you go, I want to ask a favor of you. I don't really know anybody else in New Orleans. I want the three of you and Brandon to be my groomsmen, and I want Ford...uh, Brad...to be my best man. Will you do that for me?" Kenny, Kyle, and Red thanked Jeremy for the invitation and readily accepted. Brad held back.

"You don't have to answer me right now, Brad. Let's talk, and then you can decide."

Brad didn't exactly accept the idea, but he didn't reject it either, so Jeremy took that as a positive sign.

"We'll be there for you, Jeremy, regardless of what Brad decides," said Kyle. "Now, we'll leave you two to talk it out."

Once Kenny, Kyle, and Red had left, Jeremy suggested that he and Brad sit down on the sofa, but Brad turned instead and walked over to the wet bar to mix himself a drink. Jeremy waited for him to return. When Brad meandered back over to the sofa, Jeremy signaled toward the couch with his open hand and said, "Please." The two men sat at opposite ends of the sofa like two boxers in opposite corners of a ring.

"Look, Brad, please don't be mad at me."

"Goddam it, Jeremy! I'm not mad at you! I'm mad at me! You didn't do anything wrong. I came on to you, and, God help me, I'd like nothing better right now than to rip your clothes off and fuck your brains out! But I can't, and it's tearing me apart."

"Brad, Brad. It's not your fault. You had no idea who I was. I could have stopped you, but I didn't. I don't know why, but I just couldn't. I wanted you to take me. I still do...but I won't. Truth is, I really do love Amy, and I want to spend the rest of my life with her, and I'm not going to give her any reason to doubt my loyalty. Can you accept that?"

"What about that night?"

"Well, maybe it was a mistake; maybe it wasn't. We'll just chalk it up as a once-in-a-lifetime experience and let it go at that."

"It's not that easy, Jeremy. I don't know if I can—"

"You don't seem to be having any trouble moving on," said Jeremy, motioning toward the bedroom where Brad had apparently just enjoyed a three-way roll in the hay.

Brad let out an involuntary chuckle, which broke the ice and allowed the two men to relax a bit.

"So, Brad, will you?"

"Will I what?"

"Will you be my best man?"

"I guess I'll have to," replied Brad. "Somebody's gotta keep you outta trouble."

A brotherly handshake sealed the deal.

"Can I ask you a personal question, Brad?"

"Sure. Might as well."

"Who knows that you're bisexual? Besides Red, Kenny, and Kyle, I mean."

"Well, just about everybody in the gay and bisexual community here. The ones who go to the clubs anyway. And most of the guys on the force. I don't make an issue of it, and they don't either."

"What about your family? Does Amy know?"

"Nah, I don't think Amy has any idea. Now, don't get me wrong. She's my sister, and I love her dearly, but she's always been too wrapped up in her own relationships to pay any attention to mine."

"And your folks?"

"Dad has never said anything, but for some reason I think he suspects. I don't think it would really make any difference to him, though. He's been all over the world and seen just about everything there is to see. I don't think anything would shock him. Mom? Now, that's another story. Even if she walked into the room and caught me in an orgy with 20 other men, she'd turn around and pretend that it never happened. She really does love Amy and me, but she's also extremely protective of the family reputation, and being gay or bisexual just doesn't fit into her grand design."

Jeremy and Brad sipped their drinks and chatted for several more hours before Kenny and Kyle returned to reclaim their apartment. "How 'bout we all go down to the Hellhole?" suggested Kyle. "It's Full Moon Night."

"Full Moon Night? What's that?" asked Jeremy.

"Everybody who strips down to his underwear gets drinks for Happy Hour prices."

"Sounds interesting," confessed Jeremy, "but I think I've had enough to drink. Besides, I haven't had much sleep the past few days, so I think I'd better get back to Brad's apartment and hit the couch."

"Take the bed," said Brad.

"Are you still planning to stay here for the rest of the weekend?" asked Jeremy, with a touch of disappointment in his voice.

"No, I'll come home later, but you can take the bed, and I'll sleep on the couch."

Jeremy objected, but Brad retorted, "Age before beauty."

"Pearls before swine," Jeremy snapped back.

"Hey! Is that a pig joke?"

When Brad finally got home that night, quite late, Jeremy was curled up on the bed, sleeping like a baby. A faint light coming from the bathroom cast a soft glow over his angelic face. Brad sat on the floor and just gazed at him for more than an hour before he finally fell asleep himself on the bedroom carpet.

18   The Lord's Day

Jeremy chuckled at the note that Brad had tucked into the coat of his Sunday-go-to-meetin' suit. "Help! Help!" screamed the message. "Someone left the cage door open. My ferret got out. And my vibrator is missing too!"

The Leveque clan all attended Sunday mass at St. Louis Cathedral in Jackson Square. Jeremy squirmed but took consolation from the fact that the monkey business would soon be over and he could get back to being himself again. Only problem was, he wasn't quite sure what that was anymore.

"These aren't the same flowers I sent you in the hospital, are they?"

"No," laughed Nick, as he handed the bouquet to Patty Murano. "I may be cheap, but I'm not stupid."

"I'm surprised that you're out of the hospital already. Are you sure you feel up to going to church?"

"That may be just the medicine I need."

The minister of the small country church preached about why bad things happen to good people and prayed for all the people in the community who had been touched by the recent rash of crimes. He prayed especially for a speedy recover for Sheriff Scarpelli and for young Randy Dawkins.

It seemed to Nick that every single person in the congregation came up to him after the service to wish him well. He wasn't used to that kind of attention. "It's like

that here," said Patty. "People here care about each other
as much as they care about their crops and their animals,
and that's saying a lot."

"I'd like to take you and the kids to dinner if you'd let
me," said Nick. (He had been in Wyoming long enough to
know that the midday meal, especially on a Sunday, was
called dinner, and the evening meal was called supper.
Lunch, he concluded, was what you had when you ate
alone.)

"Oh, no," snapped Patty.

The response threw Nick off guard.

"Why go out when I've got homemade biscuits warming in the oven and fried chicken, mashed potatoes, gravy,
corn, and beans on the stove?"

"Sounds great," smiled Nick.

"There's something I'd like to show you," said Patty
after they had finished their meal. "In Laramie."

After they dropped the kids off at Patty's mother's
house, they took Happy Jack Road toward Laramie, riots
of wildflowers and the scent of evergreens accosting them
at every turn.

Approaching the University of Wyoming, Nick, ever the
lawman, could not help but recall that this was where
young Matthew Shepard had been enrolled when he was
abducted, dragged into the hills, tied to a fence, pistol-
whipped, and left to die—just because he was gay. But this
was a new day, and Nick was determined not to let brutal
images of the past ruin his Sunday outing with a beautiful
woman.

As they approached the university, the Centennial
Complex rose up like a giant six-story teepee just east of
the main campus. Besides being home to the American
Heritage Center, it also houses 7,000 items in the nine
galleries of the University of Wyoming Art Museum.

"This is your work?" asked Nick as they walked through the gallery in the Centennial Center.

"Well, just these four pieces here," replied Patty. The rest were done by other students in the art department here. The faculty selected the best pieces of the past semester, and those are the ones you see here."

"Well, I'm no art critic," said Nick, "but these look pretty damn good to me."

"Thanks," said Patty, squeezing his hand and giving him a peck on the cheek.

"These rock formations are fascinating," commented Nick on one of the paintings.

"That's the Vedauwoo Recreation Area. If we take the interstate back to Cheyenne, we'll go right by there." And so they did, just in time to enjoy the orange glow of the lichen-covered rocks in the late-afternoon sun.

"How about some huckleberry pie?" Patty asked when they got back to her house, after retrieving the children from her mother's. When Patty returned from putting the kids down for their nap, she found Nick studying a very old photograph of a distinguished-looking woman. "That's Nellie Tayloe Ross," said Patty. "She was the first female governor of Wyoming, the first in the country actually."

"Impressive," said Nick.

"In fact, Wyoming was the first territory in the country to grant women the right to vote—more than 50 years before ratification of the Nineteenth Amendment. People in Wyoming like to boast that they were the first territory in the world to have women's suffrage, but that's really a bit like saying that Columbus discovered America."

"How so?" asked Nick.

"Well, women governed the Iroquois Confederation long before Wyoming Territory existed and even long before Columbus stumbled across this continent," explained Patty.

"Very—"

"Excuse me," said Patty, responding to the cries of her baby in the next room. "Make yourself comfortable. I'll be right back."

While Patty was busy taking care of her little boy, Nick continued to study the various objects displayed on her mantle. One photograph stopped him cold.

"I'm sorry," said Nick when Patty returned to the room. "I really must be going."

"Oh," replied Patty, startled by Nick's sudden change of mood. "Is something wrong? Did I say someth—"

"No, it's just...I'm sorry. I really have to go," he sputtered, his words trailing behind him as he rushed toward his car.

"But what about the huckle—". *Huh! And he seemed like such a nice guy.*

19   The Big Day

With Southern Decadence still in full swing, every cop on
the force was on duty. No leaves that weekend. So, once
again, Jeremy was left to fend for himself on Sunday
afternoon. He browsed through Ford's collection of porn
flicks but then said to himself, "Why do I need a movie? I
can see all the porn I want on the streets and in the bars of
New Orleans." So, he left the apartment and headed down
Dumaine Street, checking out every gay bar he came to.

The wedding rehearsal on Sunday evening went off
without a hitch. Mrs. Leveque made sure of that. All the
principals attended except Brandon, who had not yet
returned from Texas, but Jeremy spoke to him on the
phone, and he, too, happily accepted the invitation to be a
groomsman. Having worked all day, Ford was able to get
off for the rehearsal dinner, where he made a gracious
toast to the bride and groom. Everyone commented on
what a perfect couple Jeremy and Amy made and how well
he and Ford had seemed to hit it off.

The guys wanted to give Jeremy a wild bachelor party
after the dinner, but in deference to Ford, they kept it
relatively tame: just a few drinks (well, maybe more than
just a few), some porn flicks (gay, straight, and bi), and a
circle jerk to top off the evening.

The wedding was held on Monday, Labor Day, in the
palatial ballroom at Whispering Pines. Yes, the Leveque

estate actually had a name, and the antebellum mansion actually had a ballroom that was used for Mardi Gras balls, debutante cotillions, music recitals, and a host of fundraisers for political and charitable causes. Marie Bouvier Leveque came from "old money," and the estate had been passed down from generation to generation of Bouviers.

Pete Leveque, on the other hand, had risen from almost nothing to make a killing in the export-import business. He was now one of New Orleans' richest and most highly respected citizens.

Neither Amy nor Ford had to work, and Mrs. Leveque disapproved of their career choices, but their father encouraged them to "follow their bliss," as the anthropologist Joseph Campbell used to say.

The ceremony was conducted by no less than the Archbishop of New Orleans. The bride wore a Valentino Garavani original. Standing up with her were two cousins and three of her closest friends from college. Ford, of course, served as Jeremy's best man, and Brandon, Red, Kenny, and Kyle served as groomsmen, a most dashing entourage in their black tuxedos. Music was provided by a select group of musicians from the New Orleans Symphony Orchestra and the Loyola University Choir. The reception was catered by Emeril Legasse. The entire affair was more than Amy had wanted and certainly more than Jeremy would have planned, but Mrs. Leveque insisted that the Bouviers had a reputation to uphold.

Everything went smoothly...at first. And then the archbishop came to that standard line, "If anyone knows why this man and this woman should not be joined together in holy matrimony, let him speak now or forever hold his peace."

"I do! I can't let you marry this man, Amy!" The shout from the back of the ballroom stunned everyone.

"Paul?" Amy gasped, before she collapsed in Jeremy's arms.

20   Topeka, 1985

"What the hell did you do to Becky?" the kid demanded to know.

"Whoa, kid. Calm down."

"She wasn't at school today, so I called her, and she wouldn't stop crying. She said she never wants to see me again as long as she lives. I know it was you. What did you do to her?"

"Well, punk, you didn't man up and give her what she needed, so I did it for you. You should be thanking me."

"How could you do that to my girl?"

"Hell," laughed the bully, "she ain't no girl no more."

"You goddam sonofabitch, I'll fuckin' kill you!" screamed the kid as he lunged at the older boy, but the bully was quicker. He sidestepped the kid and tripped him, sending him crashing into the wall. The kid tried again, but the older boy, bigger and stronger, beat him to a pulp and then pinned him to the floor.

"You wanna know what I did to Becky? Huh? Do ya? Well, I'll show you, you fuckin' little shit." And when he was done, he grabbed the kid by the throat and growled into his face, "That little cunt may have been your bitch, but now you're mine, ya hear? And if either one of you breathes a word of this to anybody, I'll fuckin' kill ya both."

21   The Mysterious Paul

"Who the fuck is Paul?" Jeremy demanded to know, as he fought unsuccessfully to break through the defensive line formed by his best man and four groomsmen. He was determined to get back upstairs to the bedroom where he had deposited Amy after she fainted on the verge of becoming Mrs. Jeremy Travis. He had, of course, wanted to remain by her side, as had the intruder Paul, but Mrs. Leveque had insisted that they both leave her daughter to recover.

"Dr. Chevalier will take excellent care of her," she asserted. "The last thing she needs right now is to wake up and find the two of you fighting over her like a couple of wild animals." Ford, Brandon, Red, Kenny, and Kyle ushered the reluctant Jeremy into the study while Mr. Leveque unceremoniously escorted Paul into the living room.

"Paul Broussard," said Ford. "He and Amy were an item all through college. They were even engaged to be married. Paul got through college on an ROTC scholarship and went into the Army right after graduation. Amy had wanted to get married right away, but Paul insisted that they wait until he got home. Six months later, we got word that Paul had been killed when his Humvee hit an IED in Iraq. Amy was devastated. That's the main reason she moved to Wyoming, to get away from the memories and make a fresh start."

Jeremy fidgeted and paced for two hours, though it seemed more like two years, his mind rumbling with all sorts of questions. Finally, Mrs. Leveque descended the stairs, but she walked right past the study and into the living room. A moment later, she headed back up the stairs with her husband and Paul in tow. Jeremy ran after them, but Pete Leveque stopped him cold. "Not now, Jeremy. You'll have your turn. Please be patient."

Patient? He'd been patient for two fuckin' hours. He wanted to see his goddam fiancée. What right did this fuckin' ghost have to come back from the dead and bust up his goddam wedding? And why had Amy asked to see this asshole instead of the man she was about to marry?

Another hour passed, and Jeremy was about ready to crawl out of his skin. Finally, Mr. Leveque came down the stairs and entered the study. "Paul has left by the back stairs. Amy will see you now." Jeremy shot up the stairs and threw himself at Amy's side.

Amy began by telling Jeremy how much she loved him and how she had been looking forward to becoming his wife. Then, she recounted the story of her relationship with Paul—pretty much what Ford had already told him, except that she added what she had just learned from Paul.

When his Humvee was blown up, body parts were strewn everywhere and identification had been virtually impossible. It was assumed that Paul had been killed along with all the other members of his troop who were riding in the Humvee, but, in fact, he had been taken prisoner, and it was not until an American reconnaissance force came across the compound where he was being held captive that he was freed.

He was sent to the U.S. Army Medical Center at Ramstein Air Base in Germany to recuperate, and when he got home and learned that the love of his life was about to be wed to another man, he raced to Whispering Pines to win her back.

After all the preamble, Amy finally got to the crux of the matter. "I'm sorry, Jeremy, but I can't marry you. Paul asked me first, and I may not marry him either...I...I just don't know. Right now, I just need some time to myself to clear my head. Please forgive me."

Jeremy tried to be compassionate and understanding, but what he really felt was pissed—not at Amy, but at Paul. Or was he actually pissed at himself for not really knowing who he was, what he wanted? Though Amy did not know it, at that moment, Jeremy was just about as confused as she was.

Ford jumped at the sound of the front door slamming shut. When he ran to see what was happening, he caught Jeremy speeding away in his BMW convertible. "We've gotta stop him, Ford," said Kenny. "There's no telling what he might do."

"We'll have to take your car. He just took off in mine."

"Red, Kyle, and I came over in a taxi. We knew that parking might be a problem."

"Great!" said Ford sardonically.

"We can take my car," offered Brandon.

"We'll take your car, but you're staying here. If he's headed where I think he is, you're too young to get in."

"Either I go, or you don't get my car."

Ford felt like slapping Brandon upside the head, but he knew it would be futile, and time was running out. "OK, you little shit, but I'm driving! And when we get there, you hang close to us and don't say a fuckin' word."

"Where the hell are we going?" Brandon asked.

"Never mind. He may not even be there, but he doesn't know the city well, so there are really only a couple of places he might be."

When the five young men arrived at the Talon, the bar
that Jeremy had stumbled into his first night in New
Orleans, the jilted groom was already on his third scotch,
even though he had had only a short lead over the posse.
Burt, the bartender, eyed Brandon skeptically but did not
card him since he had entered the adults-only establishment with two cops known all too well to him.

Though most of the tourists who had come into town
for Southern Decadence had now left, the bar was still
filled with local men. The room was not as dark as the
night that Ford, Red, and Kenny had first met Jeremy
there, and it did not take long for Brandon to figure out
what kind of establishment it was.

A big, burly stevedore exited the small room known to
the regulars as the Clown Car, zipping up his jeans as he
strolled over to the bar. He was followed a few minutes
later by a young twink who looked like he must have used a
fake ID to get into the place—or perhaps he, too, had been
accompanied by one of New Orleans' finest, or by the
district attorney, or even the mayor. The young twink
licked his lips and grinned from one ear to the other as he
strutted back by the pool table. A few minutes later, he
strolled back into the Clown Car with an older black man
whose huge cock was already half exposed.

"What'll ya'll have?" Burt asked the five men as they
gathered around Jeremy.

"Beer," said Ford, thinking that Jeremy might be more
apt to listen to him if they were sharing drinks. "Beer,"
echoed Red, then Kenny, then Kyle, and then Brandon.

"I think he meant to say 'root beer'," corrected Ford,
leering at his younger cousin. Brandon started to object;
after all, he had drunk beer before; hell, Ford had even
given him beer when they were both under age. But Ford
glared at him with that look that said, "This is a cop
speaking now, kid. Don't press your luck."

Ford listened attentively as Jeremy recounted Amy's confession, if that's what it was. When Jeremy ordered his fourth drink, Ford knew better than to object, but he flashed a look that signaled to Burt to start watering down the liquor. Several drinks later, after Jeremy was too tipsy to object but not so bombed as to be unmanageable, Ford said, "Look, you need a diversion, but not here. Come with me."

As they headed for the exit, Ford noticed that Brandon was not with them. "That fuckin' kid! I told him to stick close by. Either of you see where he went?" Red, Kenny, and Kyle all shrugged their shoulders, and Jeremy looked as if he hadn't even noticed the teenager come in with them.

"Kenny, you and Kyle look outside. Red, you take care of Jeremy. I'll look around in here."

Ford navigated his way among the patrons, circled the pool table, and checked out the restroom. Nothing. Then, he gazed at the door to the notorious Clown Car. *He wouldn't be in there!* Still, he had to check. He pried open the door ever so slightly and peeked in. He could not believe his eyes. It was not the sight of eight or ten men wanking their cocks and each others' that unnerved him, but the fact that they were also cheering on his young cousin as he got serviced by the young twink.

Ford's initial instinct was to grab Brandon by the ears and drag him out of there, but he knew that it wouldn't take long for a horny 18-year-old to shoot his wad, so he waited for Brandon to exit the room and return to the bar, where he unceremoniously pulled him aside.

"Is there anything you wanna tell me?" asked Ford sternly.

"Like what?"

Ford held his tongue but shot darts straight into Brandon's eyes.

"Oh, I'm guessing you already know."

"Why don't you tell me yourself?"

"What, you want me to tell you that I'm gay? Is that it?"

"Well, are you?"

"Does it really make any difference?"

"Not to me. Question is, does it make any difference to you?"

"Whaddya mean?"

"Look, Brandon. You know I love you like a brother, and I always will, no matter what. And I know I'm a shitty role model, living a double life like I do, but it's because of that that I know how hard it can be. If you're gay, just come out and say so. Let the whole world know. It'll be a helluva lot easier than trying to hide it. Believe me, I know."

"You're right, Ford. I am gay, and there's no reason I should hide it." The teenager held back his tears as he hugged his older cousin.

"OK, enough of that," said Ford. "I need you to take Kenny, Kyle, and Red wherever they want to go and then go back to the house."

"We'd better get you home while you can still walk," said Ford to Jeremy when all the guys met up outside the bar.

"Where's home?" asked Jeremy.

"Well, for now, it's my place."

"That's nice," drawled Jeremy, still tipsy and now almost completely wiped out. "Thank you, buddy," slurred Jeremy. "Gotta get up in the mornin'. Goin' on my honeymoon."

Ford put Jeremy to bed and then, as he had done before, fell asleep on the bedroom floor.

In the middle of the night, Ford was awakened by the sounds of Jeremy stumbling to the bathroom. When

Jeremy came out and saw Ford sitting on the floor, he threw himself on top of Ford.

"Fuck me, Ford. Pop my cherry. Make love to me."

"I can't do that, Jeremy. You know how much I care about you, and there is nothing more I would like than to make love to you, but you're drunk, Jeremy. I can't take advantage of you like this."

"Yeah, I've been drinking, but I know what I'm doing, and I know what I want, and what I want is you, Ford. I want to get fucked. Please, Ford. Please love me."

Ford hoisted Jeremy to his feet and led him back to the bed. He leaned over to kiss the cowboy gently goodnight, but Jeremy grabbed him tightly and refused to let go. He forced his tongue between Ford's lips and into his mouth. Ford tried to resist, but Jeremy wouldn't let him go...or was Ford just not trying hard enough? He knew it was wrong, or was it? He really wanted this stud. He had wanted him from the moment he first laid eyes on him. Ford finally pulled back and stared longingly into Jeremy's dreamy blue eyes. "Oh, what the fuck," he said, as he fell on top of Jeremy.

Jeremy woke up Tuesday morning with a very achy head and an even sorer ass. Groggy as he was, he did recognize the lavender walls and erotic wall hangings this time. He stumbled over Ford to get to the bathroom, waking him in the process. While Jeremy tried to wash away his sins, Ford dragged himself to the kitchen to make some coffee.

Hardly a word was spoken as the two drank their coffee, but between sips, Jeremy hummed "Here Comes the Bride." Finally, Ford placed a gentle hand on Jeremy's arm.

"Have you figured out what you're going to do, buddy?"

"Do? I'm going to go on my honeymoon."

"Jeremy, you do recall what happened yesterday?"

"Yesterday? Oh, yeah. That asshole crashed my wedding, and Amy jilted me." Then, with an awkward titter, he added, "And then I got my ass drilled, didn't I? Ha ha. I guess you could say I got screwed all the way around. Ha ha." Reaching out with both hands, he pulled Ford close and kissed him on the lips. Then, in a much gentler tone, he added, "Thank you, Ford. What you did last night was real sweet. I love you, buddy."

"I love you too, Jeremy."

Then, as if reality had suddenly struck back, Jeremy observed, "Not only did I lose my girl and my virginity, but I lost the $7,000 that I paid out for the honeymoon. Sucker!"

"Maybe not," reflected Ford.

"Huh?"

"Well, you've paid for the flight and the hotel, why don't you take the trip anyway? It could be good for you to get away...let the dust settle for a few days."

"Sure, sweetheart. You wanna come with me? I can carry you over the threshold."

"Actually, it would probably be better if you didn't go alone, but I can't get away right now. Is there anybody else you could take with you?"

Jeremy just stared off into the distance.

"I have an idea," said Ford, dialing his phone.

"Brandon. Pack a bag. You're going to the Bahamas."

When Ford drove them to the airport, he gave Brandon some extra money to buy any additional things he would need when he got to the Bahamas. Then, he watched longingly as his cousin and his lover flew off together to paradise.

"Well, I guess church didn't agree with you," Ben Carter said to Nick Scarpelli, reflecting on the younger man's demeanor when he picked him up to drive him to the morgue on Tuesday.

"Guess not," mumbled Nick. And that was the end of that conversation until they arrived at their destination.

"Yes," said the coroner to Sheriff Scarpelli and Chief Carter when they met him at the morgue. "The blade on the weapon found at the scene does match the incision in the victim's chest. There's no doubt about it: that knife is your murder weapon."

"What about the prints we found on the knife handle?" asked the sheriff.

"There was one set, and they match your suspect, Randy Dawkins."

Sheriff Scarpelli paced in a circle for nearly a minute before he spoke again. "Lemme ask you...could Mr. Pipkins' assailant have attacked him from above...say, from a ledge...maybe eight feet up?"

"Absolutely not," replied the coroner.

"You seem very sure of that," chimed in a surprised Chief Ben Carter.

"Look here," explained the coroner, removing the sheet to expose the corpse of Carl Pipkins. "This is the entry wound. Given the angle of entry and the selective bruising, the fatal blow could only have been delivered by someone standing directly in front of the victim and, I would say, by someone of approximately the same height."

"Well, there goes your theory," Chief Carter said to Sheriff Scarpelli.

"Not necessarily," replied Nick. "Randy still could have jumped him from the hayloft, grabbed the knife, and then stabbed him."

"No, he couldn't," said the coroner. Then, responding to the puzzled expressions on the two lawmen's faces, he added, "The prints on the handle show that Randy gripped the knife with his thumb and forefinger up against the hilt, the back of his hand away from the blade. Holding the knife in that fashion—underhanded, so to speak—he would have to have swung upward, most likely striking the victim in the stomach rather than the chest. No, the prints on the weapon belong to Randy Dawkins, but those are not the prints of the man who stuck that knife into Carl Pipkins' chest."

After giving Sheriff Scarpelli and Chief Carter a moment to digest this new information, the coroner continued, "Don't you think it's a bit odd, Sheriff, that there was only one set of prints on the murder weapon? Not even the victim's prints were on it, and it was *his* knife. Now, I'm no detective, but it seems to me that someone— most likely, the person who stabbed the victim—wiped the handle free of prints, including his own, and then placed the knife in the hand of Randy Dawkins to throw suspicion onto him."

"But who would want to frame Randy Dawkins?" asked Police Chief Carter.

"I don't know," replied Nick, "but I sure as hell intend to ask him."

23　The Bahamas

Checking in at the hotel in the Bahamas, Jeremy explained that he no longer needed the honeymoon suite, but it was the only room available, and since he had already paid for it, he accepted it.

Brandon looked forward to swimming, snorkeling, sailing, and golfing, but all Jeremy seemed to want to do was mope around. Brandon tried to allow Jeremy his private moments, but he was also under strict orders from Ford to keep an eye on the jilted lover. Of course, Brandon was hoping for a repeat of their sexual experience, but Jeremy's heart really wasn't in it. Though Jeremy did not say so, Brandon could tell that he mostly just wanted to be held, and Brandon was happy to oblige. He really cared for Jeremy, and he wanted to be there for him—in whatever way Jeremy needed him.

Brandon suggested that they hit the beach, and Jeremy grudgingly gave in. Jeremy had brought rather plain swim trunks, but Brandon insisted that they wear the new Aussiebum™ thongs that he had bought in the hotel gift shop with the money that Ford had given him. (He also bought Ford an Addicted™ bikini as a souvenir.) In another life, Jeremy's modesty would have prevented him from wearing a swimsuit that openly displayed his bubble butt and barely contained his impressive family jewels, but after what he had just been through, modesty was no longer an issue and, frankly, he didn't give a shit what anybody thought.

He needn't have been concerned anyway. Every woman on the beach fantasized about sinking her teeth into the G-string and peeling off the threads, and every man wished that he had the balls (both literally and figuratively) to be so bold.

As they strolled along the beach, Jeremy and Brandon chatted about farming and ranching and about growing up in the country. Brandon talked about looking forward to college, and Jeremy shared the benefit of his experiences. As the warm sun softly baked their nearly naked, beautiful bodies, Jeremy's mood slowly improved. He turned to the teenager, looked him squarely in those darling eyes, and said, "Thank you, Brandon."

"For what?"

"For coming here with me. For sticking by me. For listening. For just being you. We may not be cousins, Brandon, but I feel like we are more than that." After a brief pause, he continued, "Have you and Ford always been so close?"

"Well, it's kind of complicated."

"I'm sorry. I didn't mean to pry."

"No, it's OK. I don't mind telling you. Truth is, even though we've only known each other for a few days, Jeremy, I really like you. You seem like someone I can trust, only I don't know how much you really wanna hear."

Jeremy placed a reassuring hand on Brandon's shoulder. "I wanna hear whatever you feel comfortable telling me, Brandon. You have my word I won't repeat any of it to another soul."

Something in Jeremy's touch and the tone of his voice persuaded Brandon that he could, indeed, trust his new friend.

Brandon took a deep breath and began. "First, I wanna emphasize that Ford is a really great guy, and you couldn't have asked for a better brother-in-law. But he wasn't

always that way. When he was a teenager, he fell in with
the wrong crowd—drugs, gangs, petty theft, and even some
violence. Uncle Pete and Aunt Marie tried everything—
counseling, tough love, boot camp—but nothing seemed to
help. They just knew that if something didn't give—and
soon—Ford would end up either in prison or the morgue.
Finally, my folks suggested that Ford come and live with us
for a while. 'Get him out of the city, away from all those
bad influences,' they said. 'Give him a chance to make a
fresh start.'"

"And I guess it worked, huh?"

"Mmm...not right away."

"I was 13 when Ford came to live with us, and he was
16."

"Wait a minute," interrupted Jeremy. "You mean Ford
is only 21? He seems so much older, more mature."

"Our birthdays are very close together. In a couple of
months, I'll be 19, and he'll be 22, and you're right; he is
very mature, but it came at a price."

Jeremy edged closer to Brandon and leaned toward
him to show that the young man had his undivided
attention.

Brandon took another deep breath and continued.
"Ford was mad as hell about being sent away. He looked
around for someplace to vent his anger, and he found it.
Me. He always stopped just short of really hurting me, but
he did make my life miserable for a while. Coming to live
with us was supposed to help straighten Ford out, but it
had the opposite effect. He was just as bad as ever...if not
worse...and now I was starting to slide too. My grades went
down—way down—and I started getting into fights and
drugs and alcohol."

By this point in Brandon's account, Jeremy was furious
with Ford. He couldn't believe how badly he had misjudged
the asshole.

"I know I promised not to repeat anything you told me, Brandon, but—"

"No, wait, Jeremy, there's—"

"...but I didn't promise not to rip out that goddam motherfucker's balls and shove 'em down his throat when we get back."

"But he's not anything like that now, Jeremy."

"You're telling me that he all of a sudden just up and changed...overnight?"

"Well, yeah...almost. Ya see, one day I missed the bus because I had to stay after school for detention, so I had to walk home. I was about halfway home when three guys in a pickup asked me if I wanted a ride. 'Sure,' I said. When we got to my place, they asked me if I wanted to go in the barn and smoke some pot. 'Fuck yeah,' I said. 'Let's do it.' Only, there was no pot.

"After they beat the crap out of me, they stripped me and bent me over a bale of hay. Two of 'em held me down while the third unzipped his jeans and came at me. It was pretty obvious what he intended to do, but he had a surprise coming.

"Ford heard the commotion, and when he came into the barn and saw what was going on, he charged at the guy and decked him before he even got a chance to pull his dick out. It's a good thing too. Ford probably would've ripped it right off. Even though he was outnumbered three to one, he took 'em on and whipped all three of 'em. I think he broke one of 'em's arm, and another one barely made it back to their truck. He probably limped for weeks. We never saw hide nor hair of those guys again. I'm not sure, but I suspect that that experience had something to do with why Ford became a cop."

Jeremy nodded in concurrence, and Brandon continued.

"Ford became my guardian angel. Not only did he look out for me, but he helped me with my chores and even my school work. His grades and mine both went up...a lot. He's actually very smart; he just hadn't applied himself before. When I started dating, he taught me about girls, and he always stressed that I should treat them with respect. It wasn't until after he moved back to New Orleans that I came to realize I was really more interested in guys than girls. He started showing my folks a lot more respect too. Uncle Pete and Aunt Marie couldn't believe the transformation."

Jeremy realized that he had not been wrong about Ford after all. In fact, he now appreciated him even more.

The sound of muffled grunts and moans emanating from the bushes behind a sand dune interrupted their train of thought. "What was that?" asked Brandon, though he had a pretty damned good idea what it was. "Wanna check it out?"

"No, you go ahead," replied Jeremy, totally uninterested in the prospect.

"OK," said Brandon, somewhat disappointed but prepared to accompany Jeremy back to the hotel room.

"No, really, Brandon. You go ahead," Jeremy repeated. "I could use a little time to process all this shit going through my head right now. I'm gonna take my time getting back to the room, and then I'm gonna take a nice, long, hot shower."

As Jeremy ambled back toward the hotel, Brandon turned toward the noises drawing him nearer. Peeking through the bushes, he spied two bodies rolling over the sand. He recognized them as two men he had passed earlier on the beach. At first, he had thought they were father and son, the younger one being in his late thirties or early forties and the older one appearing to be about 20 years his senior, but the way they looked at each other told Brandon that they were actually lovers, and now he could see the proof of that.

Neither man was as hunky as Jeremy, thought Brandon, but they were still a sight to behold, especially to a teenager with raging hormones. Flaming red hair adorned the younger man's head as well as his chin, chest, abdomen, and, as Brandon could now see, his genitals. He was a ginger on fire. The older man was equally handsome, if not more so, with salt-and-pepper hair, silvery sideburns, and sketchy slivers of gray accentuating his black chest hair.

The skimpy bikini swimsuits they had worn so confidently on the beach now hung precariously over the branches of a coco plum bush.

Brandon stared at the two men as their naked, sunbaked bodies pulled toward each other like magnets. Their lips met in a tender kiss. The younger of the two men gently ran a single finger over his lover's face, tracing the beautiful Greco-Roman features. He worshipped him with his eyes. He planted butterfly kisses across his forehead, his cheeks, his neck, his ears, and even his eyelids and the tip of his sculpted nose. He ran his tongue lightly over his delicious lips and then bit down on them softly, sensually. It was not so much lust as adoration, thought Brandon, but the man's hormones quickly took over, and he grabbed his older partner and, breathing heavily, thrust his tongue into his mouth. He rolled over on top of him and ground their crotches together. One was already hard as a rock, and the other was quickly getting there. The ginger dived at his partner's cock, lapping it up like a starving puppy before impaling his mouth with it.

Other beachcombers caught the moans and groans coming from the bushes, but the enthusiastic lovers did not care. *Let them listen; hell, let them watch if they want. Our love is no secret.*

"Take me," pleaded the young redhead. "I want you inside me."

The silver stallion pumped with both his cock and his hand until neither man could hold back any longer. As the young ginger lying on his back shot his own cream across the white sand, his sphincter muscles squeezed his partner's manhood tighter and forced the life out of it, sending burst after burst up his pipeline and driving him to the point of hysteria. The blood drained from their now-useless brains, and their bodies imploded into the vortex of euphoria.

Just on the other side of the bushes across the way from Brandon, three inquisitive kids beat off to the organic rhythm of Eden's primordial dance.

Mentally and emotionally processing the scene in the bushes as he ambled back to the hotel, Brandon came to the deep realization that he wanted what those two men had—not a relationship that was intergenerational *per se*, but a love that is ageless. *Someday. Someday.*

From outside the hotel room that he shared with Jeremy, Brandon fumbled for the door key, frantic to reach the phone ringing off the hook before the caller could hang up. With the water running in the shower, Jeremy evidently had not heard the incessant ringing.

When Brandon threw back the shower curtain, his face looked like bleached marble.

"Brandon, what's wrong? What is it?"

"It's Ford. He...he's...he's been shot!"

Wade Dawkins stood defiantly in the doorway to his son's hospital room the day after Labor Day. "I'm not letting you anywhere near my son, Sheriff. Not without an attorney present anyway."

"I understand your concern for your son, Mr. Dawkins. Truth is, I don't believe that he killed Carl Pipkins. Someone has gone to great lengths, though, to make it appear that way."

"Wa...wait. You're saying that someone is trying to frame Randy?"

"That's exactly what I'm saying, Mr. Dawkins."

"But who? Why?"

"I don't know, but if you'll let me talk with your son, I'm hoping that he can help us figure it out."

Wade Dawkins stepped aside for Sheriff Scarpelli and Chief Carter to enter the room.

"May I?" asked Nick, resting his hand on the back of a chair next to Randy's bed. When the boy did not answer, Wade nodded his consent.

Nick pulled the chair up beside the bed and leaned in close to Randy.

"Do you know this man?" Nick asked Randy, displaying Patty Murano's sketch of Ned Beasley. Randy turned his head and looked away from the sketch.

"Look, son. We all know that you have used drugs. That's something you and your father should probably work out, but as a legal matter, that's the least of my concerns right now. There's a killer out there, and he's trying to finger you for the crime. The best thing you can do for yourself right now is to help me catch this person."

Wade Dawkins reached out and squeezed his son's hand and nodded his encouragement. Randy Dawkins turned back to the sheriff. "Beasley. Ned Beasley. He's my supplier. He's got a place down by Harriman."

"Had," the sheriff corrected him.

"Huh?"

"He *had* a place by Harriman. His house was blown to bits last night with him in it."

"Oh, my God, no! Dad, what have I gotten myself into?" Wade squeezed his son's hand tighter.

"The good news for you, young man," added Sheriff Scarpelli, "is that you have an alibi. You were right here when it happened. So, let's continue. Ned Beasley sold you illegal drugs. What kind of drugs?"

"Pot."

"Did you ever buy meth from him?"

"No, I told you, I have never used any hard drugs." Wade Dawkins again mustered all his strength to bite his tongue. "I was never into meth, but I know he sold it. Hell, he manufactured that shit in his garage."

"Well, that confirms that," muttered Chief Carter with no further explanation.

Ignoring the comment, Sheriff Scarpelli continued, "Randy, did you ever hear Carl Pipkins mention Ned Beasley?"

"Not by name, no, but I did hear Carl arguing with Eddie once...something about staying the hell away from Harriman."

"Eddie Culver?"

"Yeah. You should ask him about it."

"Oh, I will," Nick assured him. "As soon as we find him."

A puzzled look overtook Randy's face. "I'll fill you in later, son," said Wade Dawkins.

"OK, Randy. You're being very helpful. Now, I want to take you back to Thursday night. That night in the barn."

"I told you, Sheriff, I really don't remember what happened that night. Honest."

Nick strained to conceal his skepticism. He had seen enough drug cases during his tenure with the St. Louis P.D. to know that certain drugs can induce short-term memory loss, but marijuana was not one of them. Yet, Dr. Singh had confirmed that Randy was indeed suffering from drug-induced memory loss.

"I know you're having trouble remembering, but the fact is that you *do* know something, Randy. You just have to jar that memory of yours. Let's try this: you were up in the hayloft. You'd been smoking pot, and you crashed, but at some point, you came down from the loft. Your dad found you on the floor next to Carl Pipkins' body." Sheriff Scarpelli was treading on delicate ground; he had to jar the boy's memory, but he also had to avoid leading him.

"I don't know," stammered the boy, fighting back tears at that point. Wade Dawkins squeezed his son's hand again and brushed his other hand across his son's head.

"OK, Randy," continued the sheriff. "Try to relax. Take a deep breath." Wade Dawkins served his son a sip of water from a cup. "Now, I want you to close your eyes," Nick resumed, "and imagine that you are lying up there in the loft asleep. Then, something wakes you. A light, a sound, something."

"Voices," said Randy. "I hear voices."

"That's good, Randy. That's very good. Now, what kind of voices?"

"Men. Two of them, I think. They may be arguing...I'm not sure...and then I hear a scream."

"And what do you do next, Randy?"

"I roll over to see what's going on, and...oh, my God!" the boy yelled as he jerked forward in his hospital bed, practically hyperventilating.

"What is it, son?" asked his father. "What happened?"

"I leaned too close to the edge, and I fell from the loft. I'm not sure, but I think I may have hit one of the men when I fell."

The pieces of the puzzle were beginning to fall into place for Sheriff Scarpelli. *If Carl Pipkins screamed because he was being stabbed, and Randy fell on him after he was stabbed, that would explain Pipkins' blood on Randy's clothing.*

"You're doing great, son," the sheriff encouraged him. "Obviously, one of the two men you heard was Carl Pipkins. Who was the other man, Randy?"

"I don't know," cried the boy. "I never really saw his face, and the whole thing was a blur anyway."

Nick decided that Randy was probably telling the truth. Even if his memory was coming back, he probably never really saw who the other man was.

As he rose from the chair, Nick patted Randy Dawkins on the shoulder. "Ya done good, young man. Ya done good."

"Thank you, Sheriff," said Wade Dawkins as he escorted Nick Scarpelli and Ben Carter to the door.

"He's lucky to have you for a father," replied Nick, recalling what it was like growing up without one.

Then, Nick added, "I'm going to leave one of my men here and another one at the ranch...just as a precaution. There's a good chance that whoever killed Carl Pipkins and tried to frame your son is long gone by now, but just in case—"

"I understand, Sheriff, and I appreciate it."

"Oh," said Nick turning back toward Randy. "One more thing. How did you know that you could get drugs from Ned Beasley? Who told you about him?"

"I don't wanna get anybody into trouble, Sheriff."

"Son," said his father sternly.

"It was one of the ranch hands," Randy confessed.

"Which one?" asked Nick, recalling that one of the men had cast suspicion on Randy by telling him that Randy had mentioned going down to Harriman. "Was it Vernon Wooten?"

"No, Sheriff. Not Vern. It was Johnny. Johnny Duncan."

"Can I drop you off somewhere?" Chief Carter asked Sheriff Scarpelli after they had stepped out into the hallway.

"Uh, thanks, Ben, but I think I'll stroll on over to the cafeteria and mull all this over with a cup of coffee," replied Nick.

"Well, I've got to get back to my office. Enjoy your coffee."

Nick spent the next hour or so nursing his cup of joe as he constructed, deconstructed, and reconstructed the pieces of the puzzle that he had accumulated up to that point. In between, his mind flashed to images of Patty Murano and the picture he had seen on the mantle above her fireplace. He decided to go back to Randy Dawkins' room to ask him a few clarifying questions, but he was stopped short by what he saw as he rounded the corner of the hallway. It was Patty Murano handing a vase of flowers to Wade Dawkins and planting a kiss on his cheek, the same kind of kiss he had seen her giving him in that picture on her mantle.

25   Awkward Reunions

"There's nothing you can do for him now but pray,"
said the handsome resident to Kenny.

"But he's my partner. I have to be with him."

"Are you a doctor?"

"No, but—"

"Then let us do our jobs. Besides, it looks like you need
some attention yourself."

"Oh, it's just a flesh wound," remarked Kenny, rubbing
his thigh where a bullet had grazed him. "It's nothing."

"There you go playing doctor again. Let me take a look
at it, and I'll decide whether it's nothing or not." In the
examination room, the resident, Dr. Shelby, said, "Let me
get some vital signs first. Take off your shirt." The doctor
strained to maintain his professionalism when he saw
Kenny's impressive physique. "OK, take a deep breath."
Kenny flinched as the cold metal of Dr. Shelby's stetho-
scope contrasted sharply with the doctor's warm hands
against his chest and back, now coated with dried sweat. Of
course, the doctor said nothing, but he found the manly
aroma to be highly erotic.

Dr. Shelby checked Kenny's pulse and blood pressure,
both slightly elevated, but not surprising under the
circumstances. He ran his hands up and down the officer's
torso, poking and prodding, checking for any broken
bones. He found a few bruises and some minor scratches,
as expected, but nothing serious. "OK, drop your pants."

The young doctor was mildly surprised (and greatly aroused) to discover that Kenny was not wearing traditional underwear, but an Addicted Ring Up Neon Mesh Jock™ that lifted and projected his male assets—as if he needed any assistance in that department. As he examined the bullet wound to Kenny's thigh, Dr. Shelby leaned close to his crotch to get a good whiff of his masculine scent and a good look at the genitals barely hidden behind the mesh fabric.

"Roll over on your side," instructed the doctor, "so that I can get a better look at this." What he really wanted was an excuse to pretend that he was steadying Kenny's body as he groped his bare ass. *Ooooh, what an ass! Round, firm, inviting. Ummmm.*

"Before I dress this wound, I had better check to make sure that you didn't suffer any groin injuries." The doctor did not instruct Kenny to remove his jock; he wanted that pleasure for himself. He practically drooled at the sight of Kenny's cock and balls as they fell free from the skimpy underwear. His examination of Kenny's balls took longer than Kenny expected. "Hmmm. Your testicles seem a bit swollen. Have you been exercising a bit more than usual lately?"

For the first time since entering the hospital, Kenny cracked a smile. "Yeah, I've been ex-er-cis-ing a whole bunch."

Dr. Shelby smiled back, and Kenny came to appreciate just how handsome the young doctor really was. The rumblings in his crotch confirmed it.

"Any soreness here?" asked the doctor as he massaged Kenny's growing cock.

"No, not so much that I need to lay off the ex-er-cise," Kenny winked.

"Hmmm, well, maybe a little physical therapy would do you some good. Perhaps I should check your prostate before I get back to that wound."

Kenny bent over the examining table while the doctor put on a pair of latex examination gloves and coated Kenny's ass with lubricant. Dr. Shelby inserted one finger up Kenny's ass and poked around for the prostate. Kenny twitched.

"It seems normal, but I'd better be sure." The doctor inserted a second finger and drilled as deep as he could, stroking Kenny's prostate with all the skill of a medical professional.

Kenny squirmed with delight on the examination table. "Oh, ah, ah. Be thorough, Doc," Kenny grinned back at the resident. "I don't wanna have to report you to your superiors." Dr. Shelby smiled back, nodded, and inserted a third finger.

"You're such a big man, officer, I don't know if my fingers are long enough. I may need to use a longer probe."

"Do whatever ya gotta do, Doc. Just make it feel better."

Dr. Shelby reached for the draw string on his pants—

"Dr. Shelby, do we . . . ?"

Kenny and the doctor both turned sharply at the sound of the young intern standing in the doorway.

"Shut the damn door, Cafferty, and get in here."

Cafferty stood frozen.

"Now, dammit!"

The intern quickly stepped forward and closed the door behind him.

"Shit!" said Kenny. "And I was just about to cum."

"You heard the patient, Cafferty. The patient needs treatment. Now get in here and relieve him."

"What?"

"Do you want to become a resident, Cafferty?"

"Yes, of course, Dr. Shelby."

"Then you fuckin' better start paying attention and doing what we residents tell you to do. Got it?"

"Uh, yes sir."

"Wait!" demanded Kenny. "What the hell am I doing? My partner and best friend is up in surgery, and I don't know whether he's gonna live or die. Yet, here I am gettin' my rocks off. That ain't right."

"You've just been through a traumatic experience," said Dr. Shelby, gently massaging Kenny's back. "Your adrenaline's been pumping, but so has your testosterone. Look, people handle stress in different ways. There's nothing wrong with getting sexually aroused...or getting sexual relief."

Kenny's cock twitched again, Dr. Shelby nodded to Cafferty, and the young intern gripped the throbbing tool.

The buzz of Dr. Shelby's pager broke the ambiance. "Gotta run," he said. "Cafferty, clean and dress this man's wound. And clean up yourself while you're at it. And put on a fresh pair of scrubs. I'll see you in my office later for a debriefing. As for you, officer, I expect to see you back here next week for a . . . uh . . . checkup."

"Kenny! How's he doin'?" boomed Jeremy's voice down the hospital corridor.

"Jeremy! Brandon! What are you doing here?"

"Kyle here called and told us that Ford had been shot," said Jeremy. "So, of course, we came right away. How is he?"

"Yes, how is he?" called out Red, stepping off the elevator. "I came as soon as I heard."

"He's still in surgery. Amy and her folks are up in the family waiting room. It's not good, though, Jeremy. He was hit once in the leg and once in the head."

"Oh, my god, Kenny!" shouted Jeremy, as he braced himself against the wall of the hospital corridor.

"The doctors said that if he makes it, it'll be a miracle."

"Oh, Kenny!" gasped Jeremy and Brandon.

"I think maybe we had all better sit down," suggested Kyle.

"How did it happen?" asked Brandon.

"We were on routine patrol when we got a call about a robbery in progress at a convenience store in the Marigny District. When we got there, we found two masked robbers with guns. They had shot and killed the clerk, and there was a shopper hovering to protect her little girl. Ford saw one of the robbers come around a corner and fire a shot at them. He fired back and at the same time jumped in front of the woman to protect her and the child. That's when he got shot in the leg, but he managed to hit the guy in the chest and kill him. Then, the other robber came around the corner and shot Ford in the head. Naturally, I ran to help Ford, and the shooter ran out the back door and got away. We put out an APB for him, of course, and don't you worry. We'll get the goddam sonofabitch."

"What about you, babe?" asked Kyle. "Are you OK?"

"Yeah. I just got a little nick along my thigh. I'll be fine."

"You always say that, sweetie, no matter what. Why don't you let me take a look at it and make sure."

"No, Kyle. The doctor just looked at it and said I'm fine."

"I just worry about you, Kenny."

"I know, sweetie. You think I don't worry about you when you're running into those burning buildings?"

"I love you, babe."

"I love you too, sweetie."

"Here comes Amy!" shouted Brandon, and they all rushed to find out how Ford had come through the marathon surgery.

"Hello, Jeremy," she said under the most awkward of circumstances.

"Hello, Amy."

"It was sweet of you to come."

"Of course, I came. I had to."

A surreal silence filled the corridor until Kyle, being slightly less invested than the others, finally broke it. "How did it go, Amy? Is he all right?"

Amy took a deep breath. "He made it through the surgery. The doctors have said that they still don't know if he'll make it or not. We'll just have to wait and see. They removed the bullet from his leg, and he will need some physical therapy to get back on his feet, but that's relatively minor." She took another deep breath and continued.

"As for the bullet in his brain, they explored all kinds of options—even brought in a renowned neurosurgeon from Johns Hopkins who was attending a conference here—but they finally concluded that they could not remove the bullet. It's too close to his occipital lobe, and if they try to remove it, he could go blind...or worse. They thought it would be best to wait until he wakes up and see what kind of condition he's in."

Like the lid of a vampire's coffin, expressions of disbelief descended over their faces. Totally helpless, they paced the floors aimlessly for nearly an hour until Amy suggested for the third time that they all go home and get some rest. Knowing that Kenny had a key to Ford's apartment, she suggested that Jeremy stay there for the time being, and she insisted—over Brandon's objections— that he get to Texas A&M, where the fall semester had already started.

As Jeremy exited the hospital and crossed the parking

lot with his new buddies, his mind raced to defrag the myriad clusters of conflicting thoughts and emotions that befuddled him. The electric silence that he shared with Amy was real, he knew it, and he knew that she felt it too. But was it enough? Would it ever be possible to revive the relationship that they once had? Did he want to?

And what about his new friends? He liked Kenny—a lot—and he cherished him and Red for their loyalty to Ford. He knew that they would never be more than friends, but he wanted them to be good friends... forever. Kyle made him weak in the knees. The man was pure testosterone, and Jeremy was putty in his hands. His feelings for Kyle were based mostly on pure lust, but he liked Kyle too, and he wanted to be friends with him as well. Brandon was another story. This manchild was honey and firewater at the same time. Sweet and passionate. Naive and bold. Jeremy adored him, and he had no idea where their relationship might go.

Then there was Ford, the man who had introduced him to man sex. The man who had swept him off his feet and gained his trust. The man who had shied away from him because his feelings were just as strong as, if not stronger than, his own. The man who now lay unconscious in a hospital recovery room just a few yards behind him.

As the five men approached Kyle's Explorer, Brandon quickly diverted Jeremy's attention so that he would not see Amy leaving the hospital on the arm of Paul Broussard.

Then, Brandon got into his own car and headed for College Station, as he had promised Amy he would.

Kyle took Kenny home and put him to bed immediately. He doted over him like a mother hen. As a grown man, and a very macho one at that, Kenny felt somewhat embarrassed by the attention, but at the same time, he loved Kyle all the more for it. He loved him so deeply.

At Ford's apartment, Red prepared the bed, but Jeremy continued to pace as he had done at the hospital. Then, he would sit down for a few minutes and get up and pace again. Red begged him to go to bed, but to no avail. Finally, Red got up and prepared a cup of Irish coffee for Jeremy. He did not tell him that he laced it with a tranquilizer that Ford had given Brandon to take to the Bahamas—just in case he thought Jeremy would need it—and which Brandon had passed along to Red. Now, Red concluded, was the right time to use it.

Once Jeremy became groggy, Red led him to bed, helped him remove all his clothes, and tucked him in. The four men—Jeremy, Red, Kyle, and Kenny—needed all the rest they could get. They would have to muster all the strength they could to face the challenges ahead.

26   Family

When Randy Dawkins told Sheriff Nick Scarpelli that Johnny Duncan had been his drug connection to Ned Beasley, Nick's first instinct was to go right back to Randy's bedside in the hospital and resume his interrogation, but Police Chief Ben Carter persuaded Nick that Randy had been through enough for one day and that the questioning could wait.

The next day, Nick headed back to the hospital, only to learn that Randy Dawkins had been discharged and sent home, but the trip was not wasted.

"Actually, I'm glad you're here, Sheriff," said Dr. Singh. "The preliminary lab results on Randy Dawkins' blood sample have come back. There was definitely something in his blood besides marijuana...a barbiturate."

"A barbiturate, huh? And that would explain his lack of consciousness and his short-term memory loss?"

"Most definitely."

"Exactly what barbiturate did you find, Doc?"

"Well, that's the strange thing. The results don't quite match the profile of the most common barbiturates, so I've ordered a more detailed analysis."

"So, Randy was lying about only smoking pot that night," said the Sheriff.

"Or someone slipped him the barbiturate without his knowing it."

Before Nick could ask the doctor any further questions, the announcement came over the hospital speaker system:

"Dr. Singh to ER, STAT." With the doctor now rushing to the emergency room, Nick, deep in thought over the new information, shuffled slowly toward the elevator. His concentration was broken by a female voice.

"You can't go in there," she demanded, drawing Nick's attention in the opposite direction. "If you don't leave right this minute, I will be forced to call security."

"What seems to be the problem here?" Nick asked in his official sheriff's voice.

"They won't let me see my partner," complained the man jousting with the nurse.

"I've tried to tell him," explained the nurse. "Family only."

"But Tom and I have been together over 40 years," cried the man. "If that doesn't make me family, I don't know what does."

The nurse's bureaucratic face communicated nothing but recalcitrance.

"Tell you what," said Nick to the elderly gentleman. "Why don't you come sit down with me and tell me all about it."

The man was clearly reluctant to leave the doorway, but seeing the empathy in Nick's face, he acquiesced.

"What's your name?" Nick asked the man as they settled into the waiting lounge.

"Harlon...Harlon Abrams. And that man in that room back there is Tom Jeffords."

Nick smiled gently—more with his eyes than his mouth. "And what is Tom in the hospital for?"

"I believe he's had a stroke, but I'm not really sure. They won't tell me anything."

"Does Tom have any family...other than you, that is?"

"He has a brother who has never approved of our relationship. He hasn't spoken to Tom in years, and now he gets to visit Tom, but he won't let me in there."

Nick could see that Harlon was beginning to get worked up again, so he decided to adjust the conversation. "How did you and Tom meet?"

"We've known each other since we were kids. Lived in the same neighborhood, went to school together. Then, when we went to college, we were roommates. That's when we discovered just how compatible we really were. After college, we went our separate ways for a while. Back in those days, it just didn't seem feasible for two men to be together, so we tried to play it straight. We both got married, but neither marriage lasted very long. Then, at our first high school reunion, we found each other again, and we've been together ever since." With tears welling up in his eyes, he added, "He's the love of my life, Sheriff. I don't know what I'll do without him."

For the next half hour, Nick held Harlon's hand as the old man reminisced about his 40 years with his lover. "Tell you what," Nick finally said. "Let me go talk to some folks. Will you be OK here by yourself for a few minutes?" And when Harlon assured him that he would be fine, Nick marched over to the nurses' station to demand that Harlon be allowed to see his partner, and he was prepared to employ the full force of his office to see that it happened.

"I'm sorry, Sheriff," said the nurse. "Mr. Jeffords passed away 15 minutes ago."

Nick was stunned. And really pissed off. "And no one thought to come down to the lounge and tell Mr. Abrams?"

"He's not family," replied the nurse coldly.

"The hell he isn't," yelled Nick. "Is Mr. Jeffords still in his room?"

"The body hasn't been removed yet."

"Well, you'd better see that it stays there until I get back, or I'll charge you with obstruction of justice and see how you like *your* new room." Of course, Nick knew that he had no legal grounds for such a charge, but he was hoping that the nurse didn't know that.

On his way back to the lounge, Nick contemplated how he would break the news to Harlon. When he got back to the waiting lounge, he found Harlon sitting right where he had left him, slumped over a table. *Has someone already broken the news to him?* Nick approached Harlon slowly and placed his hand on his shoulder. "Harlon. Mr. Abrams? Are you all right?" When the old man did not respond, Nick reached for his hand and then his wrist. No pulse. Harlon had gone to be with his lover.

Nick sat with Harlon for a few more minutes and then went to the nurses' station to report that Harlon Abrams, husband of Tom Jeffords, had just passed away.

"What happened?" asked the nurse.

"Well, I'm not a doctor," replied Nick scornfully, "but if I had to guess, I'd say he died of a broken heart."

Equality State. Yeah, right!

"Wake up, Jeremy! Get up!"
With the combination of exhaustion and sleeping pills, Jeremy never even heard the phone ring. Nor did he respond to Red's excitement. Or even when Kyle jumped up and down on the mattress and almost bounced him out of the bed. Not all of him was asleep, though. Morning wood flourished between his legs. His buddies had to pause for a brief moment to drink in the splendor.

Kyle broke the spell. "I'll get him up," and he did. He lifted him out of the bed, carried him to the shower (snatching a few lollipop licks along the way), and drenched him with cold water.

"Ah, ah, ah, ah! Damn, that's cold! Shit! What the fuck did you do that for?" he chattered as he scrambled to get out of the frigid water.

"Let's go, Van Winkle! Brad's awake!"

"Huh? Who? What?"

"Ford, you idiot!" teased Kenny. "Remember? Brad-Ford!"

"Ford! Ford's awake? Well, why didn't you say something?"

His buddies laughed as the clumsy cowboy tripped over his horse cock trying to get dressed.

Ford had been found awake that morning by Victor Sanchez, a very cute young nurse, who had gone in to check up on him. He had quickly summoned Dr. Galbraith, the chief neurosurgeon, who had found him to be in

"Fuck! I'd like to get my hands on that reporter and wring her fuckin' neck!"

"You and me both, buddy!"

At that moment, another officer arrived to relieve Champ, and Champ went off to find Nurse Sanchez.

"He seems to be in pretty good spirits," said Kyle, as he and Red exited the room. "Your turn."

Kenny went in first, and Ford beamed with delight at seeing his partner. As much as Jeremy wanted to get close, he thought it best to hang back for a moment, and Ford apparently didn't even notice him.

"We were really worried about you there, buddy. You took quite a hit."

"So they tell me, but I really don't even remember."

Then, Ford noticed Jeremy approaching the bed. "Well, hi. What are you doing here?"

"What do you mean, 'What am I doing here?' I came to make sure you're OK, you fuckin' idiot."

With a bit of a forced smile, Ford replied, "That's really sweet of you, Jack, but I really don't—"

"Wait a minute. Did you just call me Jack?"

"Well, yeah. That's your name, isn't it?"

As Nick was leaving the hospital, he received two calls on his cell phone, one right after the other. "I'll be there as soon as I can," he told Deputy Holloway, "but first I have to stop in at police headquarters and see what Chief Carter wants."

Nick was ushered into Chief Ben Carter's office by one of his detectives, the same one Nick had met at the site of the stolen getaway car used in the bank robbery. Chief Carter was not alone, though.

"Come in, Sheriff Scarpelli. I'd like you to meet these nice young folks. This is Bethany Rostenkowski and her boyfriend Levi Greene." To Nick, they looked like poster children for the granola industry. True to his name, Levi was dressed in denim shorts, extra thick socks, hiking boots, and a plaid cotton shirt with cut-off sleeves. His ruffled, light brown hair fell across his forehead, barely missing his eyebrows. An Aussie hat rested on his lap. Bethany wore grey jogging shorts over a pair of black leotards. A light-weight red hoodie barely concealed her black jogging bra. Her blonde hair was pulled back in a braided ponytail. A smattering of freckles adorned her petite nose, and dimples highlighted her cheeks when she smiled, which she did almost incessantly.

"What's this all about?" asked Nick after pleasantries had been exchanged and everyone had been seated.

"Well," said Ben Carter, "These folks live just off of Horse Creek Road," and they say they saw the men who dumped the getaway car." Nick wondered what that had to do with him, but out of respect for the police chief, he sat and listened politely.

"Last Thursday," said Levi, "we were driving by that stretch of road when we saw three men get out of a white Camry (Mattie O'Toole was right again, thought Chief Carter) and get into an '87 Dodge Charger."

"So, how can you be so sure the car was an '87 Charger?"

"Oh, Sheriff," beamed Bethany, rubbing her boyfriend's bare knee. "Levi here's an expert on vintage cars. He knows *everything* about them," she gushed.

"Did you get a good look at the three men?" asked Nick.

"No," the couple echoed each other.

"It's been nearly a week since the robbery," said Nick. "Why did you wait until now to come forward with this information?"

"We just heard about it this morning," replied Levi. "When we passed the Charger last Thursday, we were on our way out of town. We went to Billings for the weekend— for an antique auto show—and we just got back last night."

"They weren't home when I sent my men out to canvass the area," confirmed Chief Carter. "With no leads to go on, I sent them out again this morning, and they found Ms. Rostenkowski and Mr. Greene."

The chief thanked the young couple for coming down to headquarters and instructed his detective to drive them home.

"That was interesting," Nick conceded, "but what does any of this have to do with me or the sheriff's office?"

Ben smirked, "Just wait until I tell you who owns an '87 Dodge Charger."

Sheriff Scarpelli mulled over the new revelations all the way down to Ned Beasley's place, where Deputy Holloway had asked to meet him. As he pulled up the driveway, he spotted Holloway lying on the ground under an old oak tree in front of the foundation where Beasley's house once stood.

"Holloway, are you all right?" he yelled, running up to the supine body.

"Never better," grinned the deputy.

"What the hell are you doing, Holloway?" demanded the irritated sheriff.

"Well, Sheriff, I decided to take a page from your notebook."

"Huh?"

"Remember back at the Travis Ranch how you climbed up into the loft and lay down in the hay? That's when you found the hasp from Randy Dawkins' bracelet."

"Yeah, so—"

"Well, I decided to try a different perspective...see if I couldn't find something we might have overlooked before."

"And did you find anything?"

"Yessir, I did. Up in that tree right there," said the deputy, pointing to the huge oak, "I saw what appeared to be a piece of metal lodged in the branches."

"Oh?"

"So I climbed up there and shook the limb until that piece fell to the ground."

When Deputy Holloway handed the small plate to the sheriff, Nick Scarpelli couldn't believe his eyes. It was the VIN plate from an automobile.

"I ran the number," Holloway quickly added, anticipating Nick's next question. "It's from an '87 Dodge Charger, and you'll never guess who it belonged to."

"Carl Pipkins," replied the sheriff.

"How the hell did you know?" asked the stunned deputy.

Nick immediately called Ben Carter to inform him of the latest discovery. "Let's assume for the moment that one of the three men Ms. Rostenkowski and Mr. Greene saw was Carl Pipkins," said Nick, "since it was most likely his car."

"And the second man was probably Eddie Culver," added Ben.

"So who was the third man?" asked Nick.

"And where's Eddie Culver?" asked the chief.

"And where's the money?" added Nick.

29 Selective Amnesia

"It's called 'selective amnesia'," said Dr. Galbraith, the chief neurosurgeon at New Orleans' Baptist Hospital, where Ford was being treated after having been shot in the leg and the head during the robbery of a convenience store.

"Did the bullet do that?" asked Kenny.

"Probably not. It's more likely psychological than neurological. His subconscious is attempting to block out the trauma of the shooting. Only in his case, Officer Leveque has blocked out all recollection of not only the shooting, but all events of the past week. He may be giving himself a little extra buffer, so to speak, or there may be other memories besides the shooting that he wants to forget."

"So, what do we do, Doc?" asked Jeremy. "Should we try to help him remember?"

"Well, if he's blocking out something that's bothering him, it could be counterproductive to remind him. I think it would be best to let him work it out on his own. If he asks about people or events, you can help him fill in the gaps, but be careful not to give him more information than he can handle at any given moment. If he starts to show signs of discomfort, back off."

"He will get his memory back, though, won't he, Doc?" asked Red.

"There's really no way to tell, I'm afraid. It's all up to him."

"The wedding is still on for Monday, isn't it, Sis?"

"No, Ford, it's not."

"Oh, no, I hope you didn't postpone it on my account. I know how important it is for you."

"No, little brother. Don't you worry about that right now. There'll be plenty of time to work all of that out when you're feeling better."

"Am I at least going to meet your fiancé?"

"In due time, Ford. Right now, you just concentrate on getting better, OK?"

The next 24 hours were living hell for Jeremy. Everyone told him it would be best for him to stay away from Ford until his memory came back—although Jeremy felt that his presence was precisely what Ford needed to get his memory back. Kenny, who was put on temporary medical leave, spent practically every minute at the hospital even though he was allowed into Ford's room for very limited periods at a time, and when he wasn't on duty at the fire station, Kyle spent all of his time looking after Kenny. Red, of course, had his gym to look after, and Brandon was probably in College Station by now. And, of course, Amy now had Paul, which meant that Jeremy was pretty much all alone in the Crescent City.

Later that day, Kenny strolled back to Ford's room to check on him once again, but Champ stopped him at the door just as the head nurse, Ms. Spencer, was passing by. "He's getting his sponge bath right now," said Champ.

"Sponge bath?" asked Nurse Spencer. "It's not time for that. Who's in there with him?"

"Nurse Hackett."

"We don't have a Nurse Hackett in this unit," responded Nurse Spencer with a puzzled look.

Champ and Kenny shot panicked looks at each other and clicked immediately. They tried to open the door, but it had been blocked with a chair from the other side. Champ stepped back three paces and charged at the door with the same determination that had won him All-American honors at LSU, ripping the door off its hinges. There, standing over Ford with a pillow over his face was Nurse Hackett, A.K.A. Tommy Lee Moseby, the man who had shot Ford and then vowed to finish the job.

Champ grabbed him and threw him across the room and out the door as Kenny and Nurse Spencer rushed to Ford's aid. As Moseby scrambled to get up off the floor and make his escape, Champ went after him, but Kenny yelled out, "Get the doctor," so Champ turned toward the nurses' station as Moseby fled in the opposite direction. Once he had alerted the staff, however, Champ resumed his pursuit.

He followed Moseby down the stairs and into the parking lot, where Moseby got into an '89 Ford pickup and tore out of the lot. Champ jumped into his unit and followed in hot pursuit. He chased Moseby all the way down Claiborne, picking up two or three other units along the way. By the time Moseby turned and raced toward the Ninth Ward, at least half a dozen units were on his tail with lights flashing and sirens blaring.

They entered a neighborhood that Champ knew well; it was where his little brother had been killed in a gang initiation, but he couldn't worry about that right now. Still, he could not forget either.

He radioed to the other cops to continue the pursuit as he turned off and flew down side streets, coming up facing Tommy Lee Moseby head on. They stared each other down as they sped directly at each other. It was a game of chicken to see who would flinch first. It was Moseby. He smashed his truck into a dumpster. He tried to scramble out of the truck to continue his escape, but Champ charged and tackled him hard to the pavement. By the time the other officers, including Captain Sullivan, arrived, Champ had beaten the little shit to a pulp.

The captain grabbed Champ's arm. "No, Champ. I know how you feel, but we've gotta do this by the book." Champ glared at the captain with eyes of steel, and the captain knew he was licked. He ordered all the other men to back off and return to their patrols, and he returned to the station house. By the time Champ got through with Tommy Lee Moseby, he was nearly dead—but not quite. Champ dragged the bastard back to the dumpster and handcuffed him to the handle.

He scanned the neighborhood and saw a young man peering at him from behind a curtain in a second-story apartment across the street. It was J. T., the leader of the Spiders, the gang involved in his brother's death. It had never been proven just what their involvement was, and no charges were ever brought. Champ looked down at Moseby and then back up at the window. Then, he nodded toward J.T., held up the key to the handcuffs, placed them on the pavement just out of the scumbag's reach, got in his unit, and drove away.

"He's not breathing!" yelled Kenny.

"Get that oxygen mask on him," barked Nurse Sullivan. Other nurses rushed into the room and began administering valporic acid to prevent seizures.

"There's no pulse," proclaimed another nurse.

"Get the crash cart in here," demanded Dr. Shelby, who was just entering the room. "And page Dr. Galbraith at once."

To Kenny, time seemed to stop, as if the universe had played itself out and had nothing more to give. Dr. Shelby and the nurses ushered him out of the room. He paced frantically for several minutes before it dawned on him that he should call Ford's parents. He hesitated about whether or not he should call Jeremy, but ultimately he did.

"He's stable at the moment," Dr. Galbraith later explained to the family and friends gathered in the lounge, "but he has suffered what we call cerebral hypoxia."

"What's that, doc?" asked Pete Leveque.

"When Ford was being suffocated, the supply of oxygen to his brain was cut off—exactly how long, we don't know for sure, but it was enough to cause his heart to stop. Fortunately, we were able to get the oxygen flowing and the heart pumping again, but he'll have to remain on life-support systems for a while at least. What's more, we don't yet know what other damage he may have sustained."

"What do you mean, doctor?" asked Mrs. Leveque.

"Well, when the brain loses its normal supply of oxygen, brain cells die, and the patient may even suffer seizures or strokes. He does not appear to have suffered any seizures, but we can't be sure and we won't be able to tell how extensive the damage to his brain cells is until he wakes up." Then, he took a deep breath. "And that's the problem right now. I'm afraid he has slipped into a coma."

"Oh, dear Lord," gasped Mrs. Leveque, her husband and daughter scurrying to grab her as she slumped toward the floor.

In a warehouse in New Orleans' Lower Ninth Ward, somewhere between 25 and 30 young men, all decorated with the ribbons and medals of urban warfare—sinister tattoos and multiple scars from knife and gunshot wounds—gathered around Tommy Lee Moseby. Each took his turn beating the crap out of him, and when he would fall unconscious, they would revive him and start again. "OK, he's ready," pronounced T.J. And with that, the men pulled out their knives and began ripping the clothes off of him. Being the leader of the gang, T.J. got to go first. Moseby screamed in agony, but that only excited T.J. and the boys all the more. They laughed and spit on the animal, for he was nothing more to them than that. Tommy Lee Moseby remained a guest at the "Spider Warehouse Inn" for the next 24 hours.

Officer Marcus Champion's police report stated that he had tracked the suspect to a neighborhood in the Ninth Ward, where he had eluded capture. A subsequent report by Officer Benjamin Williams, who had graduated from the academy with Officer Bradford Leveque, stated that upon an anonymous tip, he had discovered the naked body, or what was left of it, of one Tommy Lee Moseby on the other side of a levee along the Mississippi River in the Ninth Ward. Captain John Sullivan signed off on both reports.

The coroner's report would later show that the victim suffered multiple lacerations and abrasions to all parts of his body. His jaw and numerous other bones were broken. Extensive scarring of tissue in the rectum confirmed multiple rapes as well as the possibility of sodomy with foreign objects. Evidence would suggest that all of the traumas to the body were administered pre-mortem. Cause of death: shock resulting from extreme torture.

The following day, civilians Marcus Champion and Benjamin Williams would pay a social call on a certain TV reporter.

Meanwhile, Officer Bradford Leveque, one of New Orleans' finest, lay in a hospital bed in a coma on life-support systems.

30 Sugar

After stewing in self-pity for several days, Nick finally decided that it was time for him to man up and confront Patty Murano about Wade Dawkins. Since it was early in the day, he figured that she would be home, so he drove on over to her place. When he got there, he was in for a big surprise. A white pick-up truck was parked in her driveway. The Travis Ranch name and logo were plastered across the sides. Devastated, Nick sat across the street in his car for several minutes trying to decide on his next move when events made the decision for him.

Wade Dawkins walked out the front door of the house onto the porch, turned and kissed Patty on the cheek, got into his truck, and drove off. Rather than get out of his car and walk over to Patty's house, Nick followed Wade's truck for several blocks before turning on his flashing lights and pulling him over.

"Why, Sheriff, you startled me. Is something wrong?"

"No, no, nothing's wrong, Mr. Dawkins. I just happened to see your truck, and I thought I'd save myself a trip out to the ranch if I could just ask you a few questions."

"Here?" asked Wade.

"Well, I don't mean right here," Nick feigned a happy-go-lucky laugh. "How 'bout we pull into that parking lot over there and grab a cup of coffee in Sally's Café?"

Nick began by inquiring into Randy's health, to which Wade responded that he was recuperating slowly, but effectively. Then, Nick took a deep breath, cleared his throat, and chickened out. Instead of asking Wade about his relationship with Patty, he continued to ask about Randy.

"Have you noticed anything different about Randy?"

"Well, like I told you before, Sheriff, his mother sent him to live with me because of the drugs and his behavior problems."

"Yes, I know, Mr. Dawkins, but I mean since he came to live with you. Has his behavior changed in any noticeable way?"

"Well, he's only been with me for a few months, but I thought he was beginning to settle down a bit—until all of this crap happened."

"Nothing else? Anything at all?"

"Well, I don't know why it would mean anything to you, but he was pretty upset about Sugar."

"Sugar?"

"She was one of our mares. A couple of weeks ago, Randy, Johnny, and I were riding up in the foothills when a windstorm swept up out of nowhere—like they often do around here—and spooked the horses. Sugar threw Randy. He wasn't hurt...just had the wind knocked out of him...but Sugar ripped her leg apart, and we had to put her down."

"When you say 'put her down' do you mean that you—"

"I sent Johnny back to the bunkhouse to call Doc Weatherly."

"And Randy?"

"I suggested that he go with Johnny, but he insisted on staying." Wade paused to consider his words. "I just assumed that he didn't wanna leave Sugar, but come to think of it, Johnny didn't seem too happy about having Randy ride back with him. He never said anything, though, so I let it pass. Randy and I stayed with the mare until Johnny returned with the vet."

"And this doctor—"

"Weatherly."

"Dr. Weatherly put the horse to sleep?"

"Yes."

"With some kind of injection?"

"Yes, two injections actually."

"Mr. Dawkins, would you happen to know what kind of drugs Dr. Weatherly used to euthanize the horse?"

"Pardon me for asking, Sheriff, but what does any of this have to do with finding out who killed Carl Pipkins and who framed my son?"

"Just trying to cover all the bases, Mr. Dawkins. Now, please...do you know what kind of drugs Dr. Weatherly used on the horse?"

"No, he could've used any of several different drugs. He didn't say which ones he was using that day, and I didn't ask. Randy was upset enough as it was, and I didn't wanna make the situation any worse for him."

"Of course," said Nick.

"Is there anything else, Sheriff? I'd really like to get back to the ranch."

What Nick really wanted to ask Wade Dawkins was, "Yeah, cowboy, what the hell were you doing coming out of Patty Murano's house this early in the morning?" Instead, he asked Wade to convey his wishes for a speedy recovery to Randy and sent the man on his way.

As soon as the sheriff returned to his car, he called Deputy Holloway and instructed him to track down a vet named Weatherly while he followed up with Dr. Singh.

31   The Touch of a Woman

A week had passed since Jeremy Travis left his ranch in Wyoming to get married in New Orleans and enjoy his honeymoon in the Bahamas. Of course, both were cut short.

Amy had called her school district to inform them that she would not be returning to teach. Naturally, they were disappointed, especially with the late notice, but when she explained the situation with Ford, they said they understood. She did not tell them about Paul Broussard and the aborted wedding.

Jeremy was left to cruise the bars of the Big Easy in a vain attempt to douse the pain of not only losing his betrothed, but also potentially his best man. He wanted—needed—to be at Ford's side, but he knew that he couldn't stay in New Orleans forever. Oh, his foreman, Wade Dawkins, and his ranch hands would look after the ranch, and his neighbors would check in from time to time. People in Wyoming are just like that. Still, it was his ranch, and it was his obligation to run it.

His experiences with Ford, Red, Kenny, Kyle, and Brandon had opened his eyes to a side of himself that he had not even known existed, and he liked it. But seeing Amy at the hospital again had also reawakened something in him, the need to be with a woman, to feel the soft touch of her warm body next to his. Of course, he got hit on by every prostitute in the French Quarter, and since he was such a hot cowboy, a few of them even offered their services for free, but that wasn't exactly what he was looking for. He decided to cruise the bars again, but this time he looked for bars that did not fly the rainbow flag, whose significance he had come to understand.

He found himself a nice little bar on the edge of the French Quarter near Woldenberg Park, along the river and just down the street from Harrah's Hotel and Casino. He plopped himself down and ordered a beer.

It was impossible to miss her. She sat directly across from him at the opposite end of the bar, and everything revolved around her. Her wavy blond hair gently caressed her bare shoulders. Her emerald eyes drew every watt of electricity from the room and projected it back out. She was Aphrodite reincarnated. He tried not to stare, but how could he help it?

"You OK, buddy?"

"Huh? Uh...yeah," Jeremy stammered to the bartender. "Yeah, I'm fine."

She caught him staring and broached an almost undetectable smile, but it was there. He was sure of it. She slowly ran her long index finger over the rim of her glass before bringing it to her lips and gently kissing it with her succulent, ruby red lips. Jeremy practically melted off his stool. He had hitched up his courage and set one foot on the floor in her direction when a handsome young man sat beside her and placed his arm around her shoulders. The man picked up the glass in front of him and took a sip.

Jeremy looked away, but he continued to monitor their actions in the mirror behind the bar. The man said something in what appeared to be casual conversation. The woman responded by whispering into his ear. He looked at her quizzically and whispered back. After their third exchange, the man looked at Jeremy and then back at the woman. She nodded her head ever so slightly. The man looked back at Jeremy and walked toward him.

Oh, shit. The guy's gonna try to whip my ass to impress his girlfriend. He knew that he could take the kid easily, but he really wasn't in the mood for a fight. He slapped a ten spot on the bar and turned to walk away, but the young man intercepted him and led him back onto the stool.

"What's your hurry, buddy?"

"Look, I don't want any trouble, OK?"

"Trouble? Who said anything about trouble? I'm here to make you an offer you can't refuse."

Yeah, right. Like I've never heard that *one before.*

"See that woman at the end of the bar?"

Of course, you idiot. How could anyone not *see her?*

The young man pinched his thumb and index finger together and held them up to Jeremy's face. "I'm *this* close to getting into her panties," he said, with the fervor of a horny teenager. Jeremy made a move to get away, but the young man urged him back down. "Only thing is," he continued, "she insists that she's way too much woman for just one man. No shit, dude. That's what she said." He looked back at the goddess and smiled and then turned back to Jeremy.

"Damn. She is soooooooooo fuckin' hot, I just gotta get my rod inside her, know what I mean? But she says the only way she's gonna come back to my hotel room is if I can get you to come with us."

Jeremy looked askance at the young man.

"Come on, man. You can't tell me you wouldn't wanna fuck that chick!"

Jeremy finally spoke. "She *is* beautiful."

"Beautiful? Hell man, she's fuckin' gorgeous...and hot to boot. So, whaddya say, huh?" he asked with all the aggressiveness of a used-car salesman. "You're not gonna pass up this opportunity, are ya, bud?"

Jeremy stared at the man for a few moments and then looked toward the blonde. She smiled slightly more broadly this time and ran her tongue slowly across her tantalizing lips. Jeremy didn't need any more convincing.

On the short walk to Harrah's, Jeremy learned that the woman was an attorney from Cleveland who had come to New Orleans for one last fling before getting married the coming week. She called herself Sam, short for Samantha, but having used a fake name himself when he first got to New Orleans, he took that information with a grain of salt. On the other hand, when the kid told him that his name was Rob, Jeremy accepted that on face value because he was too excited and naive to think of lying. He had just graduated from college and was in town to celebrate, which is exactly what he intended to do.

Once inside the hotel room, Rob, so proud of himself for his impending conquest, began to strip immediately, but Sam stopped him. "Not so fast, hot shot. This ain't no wham, bam, thank you, ma'am. I'm gonna give you an experience like none you've ever had before and aren't likely to have again, but you need to slow down and savor it." And with that, she re-buttoned his shirt, which simply made him all the more desperate. "Now, just watch."

As Rob stood observing, Sam planted slow, wet kisses all over Jeremy's face and neck and deep into his mouth. Rob squirmed in anticipation and rearranged the snake straining to break free of his tighty whities. After nearly five minutes of what was for Jeremy heaven and for Rob torture, Sam finally turned to the kid and gave him equal treatment. All the while, Rob kept rushing like a child struggling frantically to unwrap his birthday presents, but Sam repeatedly put on the brakes.

Then, she turned back to Jeremy and rubbed her hands slowly over his chest and arms, first outside the shirt and then underneath. If the truth be told, Jeremy was just as eager to get it on as Rob was, but he was more experienced in such matters and knew not to show it. He didn't have to, though. His dick was doing that for him, and Sam acknowledged that fact by rubbing and squeezing it firmly through his pants.

Rob's turn again. He was not as muscled as Jeremy, but he was in good shape, and his body was certainly no less sensitive. Sam's touch sent shivers up his spine. Finally, she unbuttoned his shirt...one...button... at...a...time...and placed wet kisses all over his chest and abs, squeezing his stiff tube as she worked her way around. Then, she did the same to Jeremy.

At that point, she returned to the deep French kisses, first with Jeremy and then with Rob. Then, she placed one hand behind each one's head and pulled them toward her, running her tongue back and forth between them. Once she knew that she had them under her control, she pressed their mouths together for a man-to-man kiss. By that time, Rob was too fuckin' horny to resist.

From their reactions, Sam could tell that the experience was new to Rob, but not to Jeremy. "Well, stud," she asked Rob. "How was it?"

Rob took a deep breath and confessed. "Wow! I ain't never done that before."

"But you liked it, didn't you?"

As much as Rob refused to admit it, Sam could tell that he had liked it. So, she kissed him again with slow passion, pulled Jeremy in for the three-way, and then pressed their lips together once more. She winked at Jeremy, and he took the signal to begin kissing Rob more passionately. She lifted Rob's arms and set his hands on Jeremy's waist and placed Jeremy's hands on Rob's face. She pressed their heaving, half-naked bodies against each other. Then, she moved Jeremy's hands to Rob's ass and pulled their crotches together. Rob squirmed and moaned in mock resistance, but Jeremy just squeezed more tightly, and Rob finally relented, melting in Jeremy's arms. Sam broke the two men apart and returned her tongue to Rob's mouth. Rob was left totally defenseless.

Once Sam let him go, Rob gasped for air. "Now, let's see what you've got to work with, stud," she smiled. She again took Jeremy's hands, but this time she placed them on Rob's belt buckle. Jeremy unbuckled Rob's belt, unzipped his pants, and let them fall to the floor. Then, she placed Rob's hands on Jeremy's belt buckle and had him do the same. Each man stepped out of his shoes and pants, and Sam led them to the bed in their underwear.

As they lay side by side on the bed, she slowly turned up the heat with a bombshell strip tease that would have made Marilyn Monroe proud. Kneeling between them, she massaged Rob's cock and gently chewed on it through his tighty whities. Then, she did the same through the Addicted briefs that Brandon had bought for Jeremy in the Bahamas. She looked at Jeremy and nodded in the direction of Rob's crotch, which Jeremy interpreted rightly as the signal to remove Rob's underwear. Next, she had Rob remove Jeremy's, and the kid's eyes nearly popped out at the size of the cowboy's tool. It was definitely a case of penis envy.

Sam flitted her tongue all over Rob's body—except in the most sensitive areas. Those, she would work up to. Then, she gave Jeremy the same treatment before moving down to his balls. She licked underneath and all around and took each one in her mouth one at a time. Turning back to Rob, she went through the same preliminaries before licking his cock like an ice cream cone. Then, without any warning, she engulfed his penis with her mouth.

"Oh, fuck!" he yelled, nearly tossing Sam off the bed as he shot into the air. "Oh, God, fuck! Shit! Fuck! Damn!"

With electric shocks ricocheting throughout his body, he clenched the mattress with one hand and Jeremy's arm with the other, holding on for dear life.

"Settle down, sugar. We're just getting started," she teased. Then, of course, it was Jeremy's turn. She was getting each man exactly where she wanted him.

She went back to the deep kissing, first with each one separately, and then all three together, and then the two of them together. She alternated sucking their cocks and made sure that they continued kissing throughout. She scooched their hips together, turned them facing each other, and took both cocks into her mouth at once. Both men moaned past the tongue in their mouths as she worked their pieces separately and jointly.

After several minutes, she squeezed in between them and pulled each one's head toward a breast. As they went to work, sucking like new-born calves, she writhed and purred with delight. She took a hand from each of them and rubbed them against her wet pussy. Each man inserted a finger and nearly brought her off. She rolled over on top of Rob and pressed her breasts into his face, begging him to suck her nipples together, but begging was hardly necessary. She swiveled around and sat over his face, offering him her love canal and rewarding him by sucking his cock in tandem. He went to town on her clit, and she ravaged his corona.

Grabbing Jeremy's dick, she pulled him closer and kissed him with fire on her tongue. Then, she slipped Rob's cock into his mouth. As Sam continued to ride Rob's face and Jeremy continued to suck his cock, Sam grabbed Rob's hands and pressed them tightly against her breasts.

Next, she directed Jeremy to stand on the firm mattress and positioned Rob facing her with Jeremy's long man-meat sticking out between them. She grabbed the back of Rob's neck and pulled him in for another phase of passionate kissing. Then, she grabbed Jeremy's butt and nudged him forward, sliding his cock between her lips and Rob's. Rob tried to resist, but Sam pulled him back. Jeremy slid his dick back and forth, letting them kiss each other, sometimes with his rod and sometimes without. Once Sam was satisfied that she had gotten Rob this far, she pressed Jeremy's manhood solidly into his mouth. He wasn't very good at sucking dick at first, but he soon caught on. Jeremy's moans and curses urged him forward.

Sam prepared to move them into the next phase. She lay on the bed with two pillows stuffed under her buttocks and coaxed Rob forward. This was it, he knew. Now, he was gonna get to fuck her. Oh, God. He couldn't wait. This was gonna be the best fuck he'd ever had in his short life—maybe the best he would ever have. It would certainly be the one to tell his buddies about, though he would edit out the part about the second man.

He slid his rock-solid cock into her inviting pussy and pumped away. He leaned his head toward her, but Sam intervened, pulling Jeremy toward Rob. As Rob shafted Sam's juicy cunt, Jeremy fucked Rob's face. For Rob, the feeling was mind-blowing. When Sam sensed that the two men were ready to come, she halted the action.

She turned sideways on the bed and had Jeremy lie on one side, burying his manly shaft into her love canal. Then, she pulled her ass cheeks apart and beckoned Rob to re-enter her in a new orifice. The men developed a rhythm as they each fucked her in separate holes. Sam achieved three orgasms in a row before Jeremy came in her pussy and Rob shot his load up her tight ass.

Rob started to pull out, but Sam pulled him back. She wanted to savor the feel of his thick cock. Jeremy, being more seasoned, did not have to be told. He knew how to please a woman, and in the past couple of weeks, he had become pretty damn good at pleasing a man.

Sam waited for the men to catch their breath and then, turning to Rob, asked, "Well, how was it?"

"Holy shiiiittt! My god, that was fuckin' awesome. I can't believe I did some of that shit, but it sure as hell was worth it. Fuckin' unbelievable!"

Jeremy had gone looking for the touch of a woman, and he had found it, but he had also experienced the satisfaction of opening a young man's eyes to the sexual potential that he himself had discovered only recently.

"Well, I don't know about you guys," said Sam, "but I'm famished. What say we order up some room service, watch a movie, and have another go at it?" No one objected.

By the time they had finished their supper and their second round of sex, the hour was late. Sam and Jeremy both curled up with Rob on the king-sized bed. When morning came, Jeremy awoke to find Sam gone and Rob's head nestled in the crook of his shoulder and his hand resting on his newly stiff dick. He gently slipped out from under the kid and went to the bathroom. When he returned, he was slipping on his Addicted briefs when Rob opened his eyes.

"Mornin'," he smiled broadly and with tremendous self-satisfaction. "Where's Sam?"

"Uh, well, I guess she left. Maybe she had to go back to her room and pack or something."

"You're not leaving too, are you?"

"Well, yeah."

Rob stretched out his hand and coaxed Jeremy back to the bed. "Sit." Rob sat up in the bed to look Jeremy in the eye and realized that he, too, had a very noticeable case of morning wood. "Oops!" he giggled. Then, somewhat sheepishly, he asked, "Dude... Jeremy...have you...have you ever fucked a guy?"

Jeremy hesitated only briefly, and then with a new-found confidence in his blossoming sexual identity, he responded, "Yes. Yes, Rob, I have."

"Good," replied Rob with delight. "Then you can teach me how it's done."

After Jeremy and Rob had fucked each other, they chatted briefly, and Jeremy learned that Rob had just graduated from the University of Denver and would be going to graduate school at the University of Colorado. They exchanged phone numbers and e-mail addresses.

Jeremy's bisexual tryst with Sam and Rob, though physically very pleasurable, left him more confused than ever. *What the hell am I doing? Where is this all going? The love of my life just jilted me for another man, and the first real man in my life is now lying in a hospital bed in a coma, and I'm hopping into bed with total strangers. Who the fuck am I?*

It was past noon, and Jeremy had to return to Ford's apartment, collect his things, and head for the airport to catch his late-afternoon flight back to Cheyenne. He was just about to check in at the flight counter when his cell phone rang.

"Amy! What is it? Oh, God, Amy don't tell me...please don't tell me."

"No, no, Jeremy. It's not Ford. His condition hasn't changed."

"What then?" Jeremy heard Amy fighting in vain to hold back her tears. "Amy, what is it?" he urged.

"Oh, Jeremy! It's...it's Brandon. He's disappeared!"

32   Topeka, 1986

"This is your lucky day, kid."

"Huh?"

"Yeah, that bitch from Family Services was here today. Had another kid with her. Cute little bastard. The old lady said she couldn't take another one, just didn't have room. But I told her we'd be happy to share our room."

"You told her what? I don't wanna share my room with anybody else. I've barely got enough room as it is."

"First, it ain't *your* fuckin' room, kid. It's *my* room, and you're lucky I let you share it with me. Second, you should be thanking me 'cuz I'll be outta here in a few months. I'll let you help me break him in, and then when I'm gone, he'll be all yours. Now shut the fuck up and roll over."

"Whaddya mean, 'he's disappeared'?" Jeremy asked Amy.

"Uncle Seth, Brandon's father, has been trying to call him the past couple of days, and he hasn't been answering his cell phone, so he tracked down his roommate, and he said that he hasn't seen Brandon since he first showed up. It's not like Brandon to just run off like that. Something's wrong, Jeremy. I just know it."

"Have you called the FBI?"

"No. Kenny is here on the speaker phone with me. Let me have him talk to you about that."

"Hey, buddy. Listen, I know a guy who works in the Dallas Field Office. I'm gonna call him. That way, this won't get lost in the bureaucracy."

"What can I do to help?"

"I know you need to get back to the ranch," replied Amy, "but do you think you could hold off for a day or two, or at least until we find him?"

"Of course. I'll come right over."

"No. What we'd really like you to do is head up to Uncle Seth and Aunt Cathy's farm. Somebody needs to be there in case he calls, and they could really use some support right now."

"Yeah, sure. I'll check the flights and rent a car."

"That won't be necessary. Daddy's company has a corporate jet at the airport. Just wait at Ford's apartment, and the pilot will come get you. And Daddy will arrange to have a car waiting for you."

When Jeremy arrived at the small airfield in Tyler, Texas, that afternoon a driver met him and took him to the Miller farm just outside of Kilgore. Jeremy had met the Millers briefly at the wedding, or non-wedding, but he had not really gotten to talk with them much. It would be a misnomer to call them "simple folks." They were what people used to call "the salt of the earth," good people. They greeted him warmly and opened their home and their arms to him. There was no word from Brandon that night.

The next morning, Jeremy wanted to sit by the phone with the Millers, but he knew that farms don't run themselves, so he offered to help with the chores so that Mr. Miller could be with his wife inside. Kenny called, but it was only to report that there was nothing to report. Then, he called back on Jeremy's cell phone a bit later and told him to step outside, out of earshot of the distraught parents.

"From what we've been able to piece together," said Kenny, "some fraternity plebes were given an initiation assignment. 'Fuck a fag,' they call it. They were supposed to identify someone they thought was gay and let him know that he was not welcome on their campus. We don't know yet whether these four boys actually raped Brandon, but we do believe that there was some rough stuff."

"You don't think they—"

"Most likely, he just got scared and ran away. At this point, we are proceeding on the assumption that he is alive, and we're going to keep looking until we find him, but as you may know, the longer he stays missing, the less likely it is that...." Kenny agreed to call back the next day at the same time—or sooner if he had something more concrete to report.

The next morning, Jeremy cooked a hearty country breakfast for everyone, but hardly anyone ate much. Then, he headed to the barnyard to take care of the chickens and other animals. His cell phone rang.

"Jeremy, I think we may have something. His car was spotted by the LAPD, and—"

"Los Angeles? Why would he go to Los Angeles?"

"I don't know, and I can't say for sure that he is there. All we know is that his car is there. That's not the same thing."

"Well, yeah."

"Still, it's the best lead we've had so far."

"The poor kid is probably starving. From what Seth...Mr. Miller...has told me, he had very little money, and he must've used up nearly all of that on gas. What's he gonna live on out there?"

"I hate to say this, Jeremy, but if he gets desperate enough, he's likely to do what lots of pretty young men do to make money."

"Oh, God, Kenny. No!"

"Let's hope that it hasn't come to that."

"Well, I'm not waiting around to find out. I'm getting out to L.A. as fast as I can."

Jeremy went into the farmhouse to relay what Kenny had told him, minus the scary prospects. He told them that he would go straight to Los Angeles to look for Brandon himself. The pilot who had flown him to Tyler had told him that he would wait around as long as he needed him, so Jeremy called him on his cell phone and told him to get ready. Jeremy threw his clothes together, and Seth drove him to the airport as fast as his old Chevy pickup would take them. Just as Jeremy was getting ready to walk out onto the tarmac, Seth pulled him back and spoke directly into his eyes.

"I don't know exactly what your relationship is with my son, and I really don't care. All I know is that he worships the ground you walk on...and he's missing." He gripped

Jeremy's hand with both of his and, with lips trembling and eyes watering, pleaded, "Bring my son back to me. Please."

"I will, Mr. Miller. By God, if it's the last thing I ever do, I will."

34   The Facts Speak for Themselves

Sheriff Nick Scarpelli and Police Chief Ben Carter rode out to the Travis Ranch together on Sunday morning. Nick would have gone sooner, but he needed to follow up on a few things, and he also agreed to wait until Ben got back from a police chiefs' conference in Sheridan. "I have a few questions for Wade too, if you don't mind," Ben had said to Nick. When they got to the ranch house, Randy answered their knock at the door.

"Your dad here?" asked Chief Carter.

"Yes, sir. He's taking—"

"Oh, mornin' Chief, Sheriff," said Wade, entering the foyer nearly naked. Water dripped down his muscular body, rippling through the thick mat of fur that covered his beefy chest, a dark treasure trail disappearing under the white towel that gripped his narrow waist, contrasting sharply with his sun-bronzed skin. Nick Scarpelli saw immediately why Patty would be attracted to this man. He was fuckin' hot! Nick himself had never entertained the thought of being attracted to a man himself, but in one flicker of a moment, he imagined that if he ever were, it would be someone like this. "I'm sorry. I didn't expect you," said the cowboy icon. "We were just getting ready for church."

Yeah, church. Probably taking Patty to church.

"Randy, get these gentlemen some coffee," said Wade. "I'll be back in a moment."

Nick watched the cowboy traipse back down the hallway before following Randy into the kitchen. Chief Carter waited in the foyer for Wade to return, dressed in nice slacks and a western-style shirt.

"I've already been through all this with Sheriff Scarpelli," insisted a frustrated Wade Dawkins.

"I know, Wade, but I need to hear it for myself," said the police chief. He explained to Wade the possible connection between the murder of Carl Pipkins and the recent bank robbery and how it was important for him to confirm the timelines.

"Where were your men when you left Thursday to take Jeremy and Amy to the airport?" Carter asked.

"I sent the men out to ride the range, checking for any strays or downed fences."

"But not Carl Pipkins?"

"No, the tractor we use to pull the hay baler wasn't running, and Carl said he could fix it, so I left him here to do that. I told him if he finished early, he could stay here and chop up some wood since winter'll be coming on soon."

"And the other five...were they together the whole day?"

"You'd have to ask them, but it's not likely. As you well know, Ben, we've got 16,000 acres here, so it's not at all unusual for the guys to split up."

"OK, so you dropped Jeremy and Amy off at the airport, but you didn't get home until late that night."

"That's right. I stopped at the co-op to pick up a few things, and I heard some of the boys talking about the bank robbery that afternoon. One of 'em mentioned that Mrs. O'Toole had been in the bank at the time, so I stopped by to check up on her."

Ben calculated that Wade must have arrived at Mattie O'Toole's house just after he left her there. "Mighty neighborly of you," he commented.

"Well, she was always kind that way to Jeremy's folks when they were alive."

"And then what did you do after you left Miss Mattie's house?" Police Chief Ben Carter continued his questioning of Wade.

"I grabbed a bite to eat at the Albany and then went to a meeting."

"A meeting?"

"Yeah, Ben. I'm on the steering committee for next year's Frontier Days. Ask any of the committee members. They'll tell you I was there."

"So, you got home after dark and then went to make your rounds."

"Yes, I went first to the bunkhouse, and like I told the sheriff, Marty, Vern, and Johnny were there, but not Randy, Carl, or Eddie."

"Then you went to the barn, and that's when you found Randy and Carl."

"That's right, Ben. That's pretty much the whole story."

"One last thing, Wade. Did you ever check to see if Carl fixed the tractor or chopped the wood?"

"Why, no. With everything that's happened recently, I just never thought about it."

"Where is the tractor now?" asked the chief.

"When I left, it was parked behind the barn."

While Chief Carter interviewed Wade Dawkins in the den, Sheriff Scarpelli continued his interrogation of Randy Dawkins in the kitchen. He began by asking the young man how he was feeling. "Bet you're glad to be home, huh?"

Randy responded very politely. His ordeal had obviously had an impact on him.

"How did you get along with the other guys in the bunk-house, Randy?"

"What do you mean, Sheriff?"

"Well, were you friends?"

"Nah, not really. To tell you the truth, Sheriff, I was a bit of a pain in the ass when I first got here…have been all summer actually. The guys put up with me, but they mostly just kept their distance. Can't say as I blame 'em really."

Nick couldn't help but smile at Randy's self-realization. The kid was actually beginning to act like an adult.

"The other day, Randy, you told me that Johnny Duncan was the person who had first told you that Ned Beasley could supply you with drugs."

"Yes, that's right."

"Were you and Johnny close?"

"No, not really."

"Did the two of you ever get high together?"

"A few times."

"In the hayloft?"

"Yeah. Once or twice."

"And it was more than just pot, wasn't it?"

"Johnny was into meth and God knows what else, but I never used anything stronger than weed. I know you don't believe me, Sheriff, but—"

"Actually, Randy, I *do* believe you. But Johnny—"

"Wait a minute. You don't think Johnny—"

Nick took a breath and looked Randy straight in the eye. "Randy," he asked gently, "was there ever anything else between you and Johnny?"

"Whaddya mean?" blushed Randy.

"A couple of weeks ago, when Sugar had to be put down, was there some reason that you and Johnny didn't want to ride back to the ranch together?"

Randy fumbled with a placemat on the kitchen table and took a drink of water before finally confessing.

"I…uh…once, when we were high on weed, I made a pass at him…tried to kiss him."

"And how did Johnny respond?"

"Oh, God, he was pissed like you wouldn't believe. Called me a goddam fuckin' pervert and even kicked me."

"And after that?"

"He wouldn't speak to me. Of course, no one really noticed since they all pretty much avoided me anyway."

"So, he was pretty mad at you. Mad enough to want to hurt you?"

"You don't think he could have killed Carl?"

"Maybe, maybe not, but even if he didn't, do you think he was angry enough to try to frame you for Carl's murder?"

"Gawd, Sheriff. I can't imagine—"

Having finished his interview with Wade Dawkins, Chief Carter strolled out to the barn to check on the woodpile and the tractor.

As he was heading back to the ranch house, Ben heard a thud coming from the barn. When he went inside to check it out, he couldn't believe his eyes. He rushed back to the ranch house.

"Nick," he said, breathing heavily. "There's something out here you're gonna wanna see."

When Nick entered the barn, he too was dumbstruck. There, hanging from the rafters, was another body.

35   Miss Mattie's Memories

In a great big, nearly empty farmhouse on the outskirts of
Cheyenne, Mattie O'Toole sighed as she washed and put
away the one Wedgewood dish that had held her meager
supper, which, as usual, she ate alone. With that chore
completed, she strolled over to the mantle over the
fireplace in the living room and retrieved an ornate double
folding picture frame, which she carried over to one corner
of the room. Sitting in her favorite overstuffed chair, she
flipped on the reading lamp that rested on the side table
and opened the folding picture frame.

The picture frame showcased two young women. On
the left was a picture of her only daughter Rebecca on the
happiest and sadist day of Mattie's life—the day that
Rebecca gave birth to Mattie's only grandchild and the day
that Rebecca died in childbirth. Her husband having
passed away a few years earlier, Mattie tried her best to
raise the girl, Melissa, pictured at the age of 17, just before
she ran away from home, never to be seen again.

Roughly a year later, word reached Mattie that her
granddaughter had also died in childbirth, leaving behind
a child who was given up for adoption. With the adoption
records sealed, Mattie was never able to locate the great
grandchild she never knew.

So, just as she had done every night for the past 18
years, Mattie O'Toole—known to everyone for miles
around as "The Iron Lady"— wrestled with her memories,
the good as well as the bad, and cried.

In a seedy motel off of Santa Monica Boulevard in Los Angeles, a middle-aged man carrying 40 pounds too much weight slapped Brandon around and threw him on the bed. It was all part of the arrangement. He fucked his face so hard that Brandon choked, and he spanked his ass raw and pounded his hole hard enough to tear the membranes of his rectum. Bareback. That, too, was part of the arrangement. When he was done, he wiped the sweat off his balding head with Brandon's underwear and got dressed. On his way out, he picked up one of the two C-notes he had left on the table.

"Hey, we agreed on 200," said Brandon.

"You were a good piece of ass," acknowledged the man. "I'll give ya that." Then, he stuffed the bill in his pocket and spit, "But you whine too much."

It was the fifth trick Brandon had turned that day and the third time he had been stiffed. After the man left, he got up, cleaned himself up as best he could, and went back out on the street.

Jeremy called Kenny from the airplane just before they got ready to land in L.A.

"He's there, Jeremy. The FBI agents have spotted him on Santa Monica Boulevard."

"Did they pick him up?"

"No, since you're so close, I thought it would be better if you got to him first, so I asked them just to keep an eye

on him until you got there. Mr. Leveque has a car waiting
to pick you up, and the driver has the information on
exactly where to take you."

As far as Jeremy was concerned, the car couldn't go
fast enough. The looks of the neighborhood frightened
him—not for his sake, but for Brandon's.

"In there," said Harper, the agent who met him. "Room
409."

With no elevator to be seen, Jeremy bounded up the
stairs as fast as his legs would take him. Moans, groans,
and curses emanated from the room, and they weren't
sounds of pleasure. The door was locked. Jeremy threw his
full weight against it, which was more than enough to
shatter the thin wood into pieces. On the bed, a 40ish-
looking Hispanic man covered in tattoos hunched over
Brandon, who was bleeding at the mouth. Jeremy grabbed
the man under the arms and hurled him against the wall.
When he reached out to Brandon, the man grabbed a lamp,
ready to charge at Jeremy.

"I wouldn't do that if I were you!" called Agent Harper,
standing in the doorway with his revolver pointed directly
at the assailant. "I'd haul ass out of here before I got
arrested for having sex with a minor."

"A minor! He told me he was—"

"And you believed him? What an idiot!"

The man couldn't pull his clothes on fast enough. He
was still zipping up his pants when he reached down to the
table for the money he had placed there, but Harper
squeezed his wrist so tightly that he dropped the money to
the floor. When Harper released him, the man took off like
a bat out of hell.

"Thank you," said Jeremy.

Harper winked and replied, "I'll be just outside when
you're ready."

Brandon, tears streaming down his cheeks, threw his arms around Jeremy and held on for dear life. "Oh, Jeremy. They, they—"

"I know, Brandon. I know about the hazing. Forget about that for now. The important thing now is that you're safe. Right now, we're gonna take you someplace to have you checked out. Then, we're gonna clean you up and take you to a nice hotel where you can get plenty of rest tonight. And tomorrow, we're gonna take you home to your mom and dad. They're worried sick about you, Brandon."

"I know. I was so stupid, Jeremy."

"Unh. Unh. None of that. I don't need to hear any apologies. I just want you to get better and come home. That's what we all want."

On the way to the nearest emergency room, Brandon called his folks and had a long talk. Jeremy assured them that Brandon was all right, but that he needed a good night's rest before coming come. Naturally, being his parents, they wanted him home immediately, but mostly, they wanted what was best for their son. The hospital treated his wounds, which were extensive, but not severe, and released him. Jeremy took him to the Beverly Hills Hotel and made sure that he got a good night's sleep.

Nick would not have been terribly surprised to find Johnny Duncan's body hanging from the rafters in the barn. He never expected to find Marty Hitchins'. When they cut him down, they found a note in the pocket of his jeans. He confessed to the bank robbery and wrote that with Carl and Eddie both dead and with the money gone, he had nothing left to live for. He feared that he would be caught and vowed never to go back to jail. *'Back' to jail?* The note said nothing about killing Carl Pipkins.

"Well, if he didn't kill Carl, who did?" asked Chief Carter.

"I'm not sure," said Nick, but I think it's time we had another chat with Vernon Wooten and Johnny Duncan." As they headed for the bunkhouse, one of the white pickups owned by the Travis Ranch came flying around the corner and nearly clipped them as it sped away from the ranch. Ben raced for his police cruiser with Nick hot on his tail, showing absolutely no evidence of his prior injuries. Looking back to see if the cops were still chasing him, the driver of the pickup did not see the car approaching from the opposite direction until it was nearly upon him. Swerving to avoid the oncoming car, he flipped over into a ditch beside the road.

Nick Scarpelli and Ben Carter arrived on the scene just as Deputy Holloway was pulling a stunned Johnny Duncan out of the capsized truck. "Cuff him," yelled the sheriff.

"What the hell are you doing here, Holloway?" Sheriff Nick Scarpelli asked back at the ranch house.

"I found out something about the bank robbers that I thought you and Chief Carter would want to know. I've been looking into their backgrounds, and it turns out that Carl Pipkins, Marty Hitchins, and Eddie Culver spent some time in the same foster home in Topeka. Marty even spent some time in juvie. We couldn't get this information before because the juvenile records were sealed. Once Carl was dead, though, I was able to track down the foster parents. They told me that all three of them were a handful but that Carl, being the oldest, controlled the other two—mostly for his benefit. Maybe that's what Carl and Eddie argued about."

"So, did Johnny kill Carl?" asked Wade Dawkins when the lawmen returned from questioning Johnny Duncan and Vern Wooten in the bunkhouse.

"Johnny lawyered up before we could get the complete story out of him," replied Nick, "but here's what I think. Carl Pipkins was a very domineering man. Marty and Eddie both resented it, but Eddie couldn't get away from him. Marty, on the other hand, came here to the Travis Ranch to do just that. Unfortunately, Carl tracked him down and threatened to expose his criminal record unless he joined him and Eddie in the bank robbery."

Police Chief Carter picked up the story at that point. "On Wednesday evening before Labor Day, Carl Pipkins disconnected the tickler wire from the ignition switch and the starter solenoid on the tractor and reported to you, Wade, that the tractor wasn't running. He said he could fix it. That gave him an excuse to stay behind while the other men rode the range. Marty and Eddie split up from the rest of the boys and circled back to the ranch just in time to meet up with Carl. The three of them went into town, stole the Camry, parked Carl's Charger up by Horse Creek

Road, went into town and robbed the bank, drove back out to Horse Creek Road to ditch the stolen car and retrieve the Charger, and then came back here to the ranch."

"But why did they come back here?" asked Randy.

"By ditching the getaway car north of the city, they hoped to make us think that they had gone north. Carl probably figured that if they came back to the ranch for a few days, they would be much less likely to draw suspicion. Maybe Eddie didn't like that idea. Maybe he wanted to get the hell out of here immediately. He and Carl argued about it, Eddie pulled Carl's knife on him, and killed him. Then, in a panic, he hightailed it out of here. My guess is that he took the money with him, but, being a dope addict, he had to make one last run to Ned Beasley's place."

"So, where's the money now?" asked Randy.

"My guess is that it got burned to a crisp along with the Charger and everything in it," said Nick.

"Incidentally," interjected the police chief, "drugs could be what Carl and Ned were arguing about in back of the Conestoga that Saturday night. Carl was telling Ned to stay the hell away from Eddie and stop supplying him with drugs. Not that Carl really cared much about Eddie's health, but he didn't want anything or anybody controlling Eddie but him."

"So, Eddie killed Carl and framed Randy?" asked Deputy Holloway.

"I don't think so," replied Sheriff Scarpelli. "That wouldn't explain why Johnny was in such an all-fired hurry to get away from here. No, I suspect that when we get the full story out of him, we'll find that Johnny went into the barn after Eddie took off. Maybe he went there looking for Randy, or maybe he had seen Eddie and Carl going into the barn and Eddie taking off in the Charger. Regardless, he got there just in time to see Randy roll off the loft and land on top of Carl's dead body.

"Johnny was already pissed with Randy, so he saw this as his opportunity to get his revenge. He had been lacing Randy's marijuana with sodium pentobarbital, which would explain Randy's delirium and loss of memory. Sodium pentobarbital is one of the drugs that Dr. Weatherly used to euthanize horses, and my guess is that Johnny pinched some from him when the doctor came out to put Sugar down a couple of weeks ago. When that wasn't enough, Johnny pulled the knife from Carl's chest, wiped it clean, cradled it in Randy's hand, and let it fall to the ground."

"Wait a minute," objected Wade Dawkins. "What did Johnny have against Randy?"

"I think I'll let Randy explain that to you, Mr. Dawkins," replied Nick.

After everyone had cleared out, Wade Dawkins sat down in the den with his son Randy. "Why would your mother tell me that she was sending you back to me because you had a drug problem?" asked Wade.

"Well," Randy began tentatively. "I guess technically I do—if you consider a little pot to be a drug problem," he scoffed. "But the truth, Dad, is that Mom just couldn't handle the fact that I'm gay. I dunno, maybe *you* can't either," cried the teenager, preparing to storm out of the room.

"Now wait just a goddam minute," demanded Wade. "Who says I can't handle it? Now, you just march right back here, young man. Sit your little ass back down, and let's talk about this."

Brandon slept until nearly 11:00 a.m. on Monday morning, when Jeremy had brunch delivered to the room, and then he slept again until 2:30. Finally, the driver took them to the airport.

"What about my car?" asked Brandon.

"Don't worry about that, Mr. Miller," said the driver. "Mr. Leveque is taking care of everything."

On the plane, Jeremy watched Brandon as he slept.

Finally, he slowly leaned over and gently kissed him on those sweet, innocent lips.

"I'm sorry. I shouldn't have woken you."

"Mmmmmm. No, that was wonderful. What a way to wake up. Do it again."

Jeremy kissed him again, and Brandon grappled onto his head to prevent him from giving up. When Jeremy finally managed to break the grip, he said, "Whoa, stud. You've been through a lot lately. I don't want you to strain yourself."

When the plane landed at the airport in Texas, the Millers, of course, met them and were shocked to see the marks and bruises on their son's face. He did not tell them about the bruises on the rest of his body, but they no doubt imagined. Seth Miller pulled Jeremy aside. "What happened to my boy, Jeremy?"

"We really don't know all the details, Mr. Miller, and right now it's probably better that we don't. If Brandon wants us to know, he'll tell us in his own due time. The important thing now is that he's home, and he's gonna be OK. You have my word on that."

At that moment, a familiar car pulled up alongside the plane on the tarmac, and Brandon and Jeremy were equally shocked to see who stepped out to greet them.

"Amy! That was so sweet of you to come," said Brandon.

"I just had to make sure you were OK and to bring you something."

"What's that?"

Handing him the keys to Ford's BMW, which she had driven up from New Orleans, she said, "We want you to take care of Ford's car until he's well again."

"Is he out of the coma?" Brandon asked excitedly. "No. No. Not yet...but he will be," she assured him, no doubt trying to reassure herself as well.

"Then, he'll need these," he said, handing the keys back to her.

"Yes, when he's ready. But we can't just let the car sit. It's not good for it. Somebody needs to look after it, and we, the family, talked it over and decided that it should be you. Take it, Brandon. You'll be doing it for Ford." When she put it that way, how could he refuse?

As they started to leave, Amy headed toward the plane. "Aren't you coming back to the house with us?" asked Brandon.

"No. I'm going to have Mike and Tony fly me back to New Orleans. I think you need some rest right now, but I'll see you again soon. Promise."

She turned back and kissed him gently on the cheek.

She wanted to hug him, but she could tell that he was probably sore all over, and she didn't want to hurt him. As she was walking back to the plane, Jeremy called out, "Hold up, Amy. I'm coming with you."

"Oh?"

"I've got to see Ford."

"Jeremy. I don't know if that's—"

"I'm going to see him, Amy, and that's final!" Jeremy's take-charge personality was one of the things that had initially drawn her to him.

"All right, then. Let's not keep the pilots waiting."

Jeremy assured Brandon that he would be back, and then he got on the plane with Amy.

On the way back to New Orleans, Amy informed Jeremy that she had decided to marry Paul Broussard. Though the news did sting somewhat, it did not shock him. He wished her every happiness, and he genuinely meant it.

"Jeremy, I need to ask you something." "What's that?"

"Is Ford gay?"

"Why do you ask...and why would you ask *me*?" "Well, I guess I never paid any attention before, but

now that I look back, I think the signs were there all along. So, is he?"

"What makes you think I would know?" "Because you and Ford are more than just new

acquaintances, aren't you? I'm not judging, Jeremy—either him or you—but it does seem to me that he showed more concern about you after I stopped the wedding than would normally be the case, and even though I know how kind you are, you have shown more concern about him since he was shot than I would expect from a casual acquaintance. You became more than friends, didn't you?"

After taking a deep breath, Jeremy explained, "First, Ford is bisexual. He loves men and women both, and they love him too. He's a hard man not to love." Amy nodded in agreement.

"Second, he taught me some things about myself that I had never realized before. I swear to you, Amy, up until we arrived in New Orleans, I had never been with a man in my entire life. In fact, the first night Ford and I were together, we didn't even know who the other one was. He had no idea I was the guy about to marry his sister, and I had no idea he was my future brother-in-law. Had we known, we certainly wouldn't have done it, and we didn't do anything again until after you called off the wedding. But, to answer your question, yes, Ford and I did have sex, and, frankly, I think I was starting to fall in love with him."

"Well, just so there will be no misunderstanding," stated Amy, "when Ford recovers, and I know he will, I hope that the two of you get back together. I know more than anyone how terrific you both are. I want only the best for both of you, and if that would make you happy, you will have my blessing."

Amy's statement stunned Jeremy a bit, but he thanked her and gave her a friendly, platonic kiss.

Amy instructed the driver who met them at the New Orleans International Airport to take them directly to Baptist Hospital, where Mr. and Mrs. Leveque were sitting with Ford. Mrs. Leveque balked at the idea of letting Jeremy see Ford, but Amy insisted, "It can't do any harm, Mother, and it might do some good. Besides, he's earned the right." Mrs. Leveque assumed that Amy was talking about Jeremy's successful efforts to bring Brandon back from Los Angeles, and Amy did not explain that that was only part of her reasoning.

While the Leveques went home to get some much-needed rest, Jeremy spent the rest of the night at Ford's side. Holding his hand as his lover lay in a coma, Jeremy told Ford...uh, Brad...about how he had run into him at the leather bar and experienced things that he had never known before. He reminded him of how they had fought off the two muggers they had encountered on their way to Brad's apartment, and he laughed as he recounted how shocked they both were at discovering who they really were.

He did not mention that the wedding to his sister had been called off—he did not want to upset him—but he did describe in graphic detail the night they had made love. He told him about how he had flown back from his "honeymoon" the minute he had heard about the shooting. He omitted the part about how Tommy Lee Moseby had suffocated him, sending him into a coma, but he did assure him that the man who had shot him in the convenience store had gotten his just reward.

He also did not tell him about Brandon's hazing at A&M and his subsequent flight to Los Angeles, but he did tell him that the entire ordeal of the past few days had brought Brandon and him closer. He recited the chron-ology of all these events, but mostly, he told him how much he loved him and how important it was for him to wake up and recover so that they could be together again.

Of course, being in a coma, Brad heard none of this.

There was so much Jeremy wanted to say to Brad, but with the late-summer sun slowly rising over the Crescent City, he ran out of energy long before he ran out of sentiments. Physically and emotionally exhausted, he rested his head against Brad's hand and let the tears flow.

"Why are you crying?"

At first, Jeremy thought one of the doctors or nurses had caught him in an awkward moment, but then he looked up to discover that there was no one in the room but Brad and him.

39   Nick Makes a Move

"For an interim sheriff, you've been awfully busy, mister."

Nick Scarpelli laughed, something he hadn't done in a while. "It's good to see you again, Patty. Do you mind if I come in?"

"I must admit, I'm surprised to see you, Nick," said Patty after they had sat down on her living room sofa. "After you left my house so abruptly a week ago, I thought I must've done something really bad to turn you off."

"Yeah, that's why I'm here...to explain that."

"I'm listening."

"Well, as you know, I've been investigating the crimes out at the Travis Ranch, and since Wade Dawkins was one of the principal parties involved in that investigation, I thought it best that I not get involved with you... considering your relationship with Wade and all, but now—"

"My relationship with Wade? What the hell are you talking about?"

"Patty, I saw the picture of the two of you on your mantle, and I've seen you kissing, so, naturally, I just assumed that you were—"

"Sleeping together?"

"Well, I was going to say, 'dating,' but—"

"Nick, Wade and I are not dating. All he did was marry me."

"Marry you? Wade Dawkins is your husband?"

"No, you fool! Wade is a deacon at my church. When my husband and I got married, we didn't have a minister.

In cases like that, Wyoming law allows a congregation to designate someone to perform wedding ceremonies, and that's what Wade did."

"But what was he doing at your house Thursday morning?"

"Thursday morning? How did you know about that?"

"I came by to talk to you then, but when I saw Wade coming out of your house, I...well...I—"

"Oh, never mind. Well," she sighed, "you've heard of Mattie O'Toole? She's an icon in this town, a direct descendant of Nellie Tayloe Ross." Nick glanced up at the picture of the former governor on Patty's mantle. "Miss Mattie was staying at my place for a few days while some work was being done on her house. She had forgotten her medicine, so Wade picked it up and brought it over to her. She doted on the Travises, and when they died, Wade took it on himself to look after her."

"Oh, my God, Patty. I...I—"

"Nick Scarpelli! I do believe that you were jealous."

"No, I just—"

"Oh, shut up, you sweet man, and kiss me."

And so he did, but when he tried to go further, Patty startled him.

"I'm sorry, Nick. I thought I could do this, but I just can't."

"Patty, what's the matter?"

"I really like you, Nick, but you're just here on a short-term assignment. The elections are coming up in November, and once we have a new sheriff, you'll be going back to the academy in Douglas, and I'll probably never see you again. I thought we could just have a little fun, and then it would all be over, and that would work just fine if I didn't really care that deeply about you. But I do care for you, Nick. A lot. And I don't think I can do this and just walk away from it."

"Are you quite finished?" Nick chided.

"Huh?"

"Maybe this will change your mind," said Nick, flashing a piece of paper he had drawn out of his shirt pocket.

"What's this?" asked Patty, opening up the folded document. "Is this...oh, my God! Nick, are you really?"

"Yep, I went down to the courthouse yesterday and filed the papers to run for sheriff."

"Oh, Nick. That's wonderful," she exclaimed. Then, just as quickly, she pulled back again. "But Nick, are you sure you really want to do this—especially after the week you've had?"

"Well, it has been quite a week, I'll admit, but it's also made me realize just how much I miss real police work. I think I can do some real good here, and hopefully, not every week will be like this one has been. I talked to Ben Carter, and he said he would endorse me, but I'm gonna need some campaign posters. You wouldn't happen to know where I can find a good commercial artist, would you?"

"Oh, my God, Brad! You're awake!" screamed Jeremy.

"So, why are you crying?" Brad asked again.

"Nothing, buddy. It's nothing."

After pressing the nurses' call button and phoning Amy with the good news, Jeremy went back to chatting with Brad.

The cowboy and the cop exchanged pleasantries for a few minutes before Brad said, "I don't know why...I hardly know you...but for some strange reason I feel a special bond between us."

"It doesn't matter right now," replied Jeremy, fighting to hold back the emotions rampaging inside him.

When Amy and her folks arrived, Jeremy stepped out to get a cup of coffee and make some phone calls. First, he called the Millers to let them know about Brad and to check up on Brandon. "He's a bit shaken," reported Seth Miller, "but I think he's improving. I've never seen anybody eat so much in my entire life," he chuckled.

Then, Jeremy called the ranch to see how things were going there. "Oh, everything's fine," said Wade. "We're gonna have to find some new ranch hands, but—"

"Why would we need new ranch hands?" asked Jeremy. "Those new guys didn't work out?"

"No, they didn't," replied Wade. "I'll fill you in when you get home."

"Well, no matter," said Jeremy. "I may just have a solution to that problem myself."

Of course, Jeremy also called Kenny to alert him, Kyle, and Red of the good news about Brad, and the three of them immediately hauled ass over to the hospital.

Brad recuperated quickly over the next couple of days.

"He's going to need some physical therapy for that leg," said Dr. Chevalier, the Leveque's primary family physician, "and there's still the matter of that bullet in his brain. Dr. Galbraith will want to monitor that situation carefully to decide if and when to remove it. At this point, however, I see no reason he should not be allowed to go home as long as he takes it easy."

"Wait," said Jeremy, as the Leveques were making preparations to take their son home. Turning to the patient, Jeremy said, "Brad, I have a proposition for you."

Marie Bouvier Leveque pitched a royal fit when Jeremy suggested that her son go back to Wyoming with him, but when Jeremy explained how much he would be needed there, Brad agreed, and Pete and Amy Leveque persuaded the matriarch that the move would be good for him.

The next morning, Jeremy and Ford, accompanied by two of the biggest stevedores from the city, flew north on Pete Leveque's company plane, but they weren't headed directly for Wyoming. "We need to stop in Texas to pick up a couple of things," said Jeremy. After Jeremy and Brad got off the plane, it set course for College Station with the two stevedores on board.

In the morning, as he had done once before, Jeremy cooked a big country breakfast for everyone, only this time everyone—especially Brandon and even Brad—ate heartily, and Jeremy had to scramble up a second batch of country bacon and farm-fresh eggs. After breakfast, Mrs. Miller finally asked the big question, "Shouldn't you be getting ready to go back to school, son?"

"I can't go back there, Mama. I know you and Dad have worked hard to send me to school, and I'm sorry to disappoint you, but I just can't go back there."

"You haven't disappointed us, son, but what do you plan to do?" asked Mr. Miller.

"I don't know, Dad," Brandon responded with growing trepidation. "I just don't know."

"Well, I do!" asserted Jeremy. "You're coming back to Cheyenne with Brad and me."

Carol Miller was just as stunned as Brandon was. Seth Miller was also surprised, but not quite as much.

"Jeremy, thanks, but I'll be fine, and I can't take your charity."

"Who said anything about charity? I just found out that we're short-handed at the ranch. You think you had chores here, you just wait 'til I put you to work on my ranch. You'll be begging to come back to your folks, but they won't let you."

"And why wouldn't we take our son back?" asked Mrs. Miller indignantly.

"Because he'll also be in school."

"Jeremy, I—"

"I know you're not ready to go back to school right now, but come January, you're going to enroll at the University of Wyoming. Laramie is just about the same distance from my ranch as Cheyenne, and you'll have no problem driving back and forth in that slick BMW out there. What's more, they have an animal science program that's just as good as, if not better than, A&M's."

"But won't it be too late?"

"I've got friends there. You just let me take care of that."

Cathy Miller started to express reservations, but her husband, having somewhat more insight into Jeremy's relationship with his son, interrupted: "I think that's an excellent idea. I'll help you pack in the morning."

"Seth!" she gasped, but seeing the excitement on Brandon's face, something she had not seen since he was first accepted at A&M, she had to relent. "Oh, all right. But on one condition, young man. I expect to see you back here for Thanksgiving and Christmas."

"We'll be back for Thanksgiving," replied Jeremy, but I'd like you to think about coming up to the ranch for Christmas if you would. Wyoming is really beautiful that time of the year."

"Oh, well, I—"

"We'll think about it, Jeremy," replied Seth. "Won't we, dear?"

"Well, I...I don't...yes, yes, I don't know why not! Yes, we'll think about it!"

Brandon grabbed his mother to give her a big hug but then winced at the sore spots that remained on his body. Then, he ran off to his room to begin packing for the trip. The cowboy, the cop, and the college kid left early the next morning with Brandon driving Ford's BMW.

In northern Oklahoma, they pulled off of I-35 to get gas and grab a bite to eat at a Pilot Truck Stop. "Who's the second most popular guy at a nudist camp?" asked one of the amiable truck drivers sitting across from them in the truck stop cafe.

"I don't know," answered Jeremy. "Who's the second most popular guy at a nudist camp?"

"The guy who can bring you a dozen donuts with his hands full!" the man howled at his own joke. Jeremy and Brandon laughed along politely.

"Who's the *most* popular guy at a nudist camp?" the trucker followed up with Brad.

"I don't know," Brad humored him. "Who's the *most* popular guy at a nudist camp?"

"The guy who can eat the last donut!" The man bellowed at his own cleverness.

After a few brief moments of chit-chat, the trucker's partner asked, "So, what do you do up in Cheyenne?"

"I deliver donuts," quipped Jeremy, which caused the truckers to laugh so hard that one of them nearly spit up his coffee through his nose. Once the laughter had subsided, Jeremy added, "Baker's dozen."

And after the next round of belly laughs died down, Brandon added, "And I'm the guy who eats the last one!"

The men all laughed raucously once more. "Damn, when I finish this meatloaf plate, I think I'm gonna be ready for some dessert myself. How 'bout you, Bo? You got room for dessert?" he asked with a wink.

"You know me, Tex. I've always got room for dessert," Bo snickered.

"Thanks, guys," said Jeremy, completely catching the nuance. Holding Brad's and Brandon's hands, he added, "but I've got all the sweets I can handle right here."

41   Bullet

Once they arrived at Jeremy's Wyoming ranch, Jeremy
thanked his foreman, Wade Dawkins, for all of his work
during his extended absence, and he made a mental note to
reward him with a generous Christmas bonus. He also
introduced Wade and Randy to Brad and Brandon,
explaining that the younger man would be working the
ranch with them as soon as he was all healed from the
wounds he had suffered "in an automobile accident." The
Dawkinses—and even Vern Wooten—fell in love with
Brandon and Brad immediately and took them under their
wings, and Randy took a special liking to Brandon.

The next day, as Brandon and Randy tossed the
football around in the front yard, Jeremy and Wade sat on
the front porch, bringing each other up to date on their
recent experiences, though Jeremy spared his foreman
some of the more salacious details of his past two weeks.

"Could I ask a favor of you, Jeremy?"

"Of course, Wade. You know you can."

"It's Randy. I really don't care that he's gay, but I'm
new to this, and I'm just not sure how to talk to him about
it. Do you think you could—"

"Just be his father, Wade. That's all he wants from you.
Of course, I'll talk to him any time he wants, but to be
perfectly honest with you," said Jeremy, nodding toward

the two young men in the yard, "it looks to me like Randy has already found his confidant."

"Oh," asked Wade, "so Brandon is also—"

"Yep," replied Jeremy. "Out and proud."

"Hitch up, men," Wade called to Jeremy, Randy, and Brandon. "We can't keep Mrs. O'Toole waiting. Jeremy and Wade had decided that it would be good for Brandon and Randy to spend some time volunteering to help other people in the community. "It'll do them some good to get their minds off of their own problems and focus on helping others," they agreed, and they could think of no better place to start than with Miss Mattie O'Toole. So, they loaded into the truck to drive over to her house and introduce the boys to her.

As they stepped up on Miss Mattie's porch, Jeremy turned to Brandon, "Oh, Brandon, I left a bag of stuff for Miss Mattie in the truck. Would you go get it for me?" As Brandon ran back to the truck, the rest of the men entered the house, which smelled of cinnamon oatmeal cookies baking in the oven. "Such a fine-looking boy," the lady commented on meeting Randy. "Where's the other one?"

"Brandon just ran back to the truck for a minute. He'll be here directly."

"Well, you men make yourselves comfortable here in the living room while I go to the kitchen and pull the cookies out of the oven." Without any prodding at all, Randy snapped to the occasion, "Let me help," making his dad proud. Miss Mattie graciously accepted the offer, more because she relished the company of the "fine young man" than from any actual need for his help.

With Miss Mattie and Randy in the kitchen, Brandon entered the house and laid the bag on the floor next to

Jeremy. Thinking that it would be impolite to sit down before the lady of the house returned, he coasted over to the fireplace and leaned against the mantle.

As the lively grandmother strolled back into the living room carrying a tray of cookies, Randy trailing close behind, she looked up, caught a glimpse of Brandon by the mantle, dropped the silver tray, and gasped, "Oh, my lord!"

The octogenarian had no reservations about standing up to a couple of bank robbers, but the sight of Brandon completely threw her for a loop. Once she recovered enough to speak, she pointed to the framed pictures on the mantle and directed Brandon, "Bring me those photographs, young man." As Brandon complied, as politely as he could amid the confusion, Mattie O'Toole motioned for everyone to gather around, and once they had, she turned the frame around and held the pictures of the beautiful young ladies up to Brandon's face."

"Oh, my god, Brandon," gulped Randy. "They look just like you. They could be your sisters, bro."

"Or his mother and grandmother," panted Wade. "Miss Mattie, do you really think...could they be...could Brandon be Melissa's son?"

Once Miss Mattie recounted how her granddaughter had run away when she got pregnant and Brandon explained to the elderly lady that his birth mother had given him up for adoption in Texas, everyone pitched in to reconstruct the timeline and piece together the possibility.

A couple of weeks later, Brandon received the results of the DNA test that Nick Scarpelli had arranged. Positive. Brandon was indeed Miss Mattie's long-lost great grandson, the heir to her ranch, and a direct descendant of Wyoming's first female governor.

Brandon moved into the O'Toole farmhouse, which would be his one day, and he took Randy with him. The two young men took turns looking after Miss Mattie, getting the farm back in operating condition, and working on the Travis ranch as well. Their days were long and hard, but neither young farmer/rancher had ever been happier.

Shortly thereafter, Brandon received an E-mail from Neil, his short-term roommate at A&M. The note informed him that Omega Zeta Mu fraternity had folded because it had lost too many members and could no longer attract new pledges. Apparently, the fraternity's president, the pledge master, and four pledges had missed nearly every one of their classes and had to drop out of school. When Brandon relayed this news to Jeremy, he flashed on the two stevedores from New Orleans who had flown on to College Station after dropping him off in Tyler, but he thought it best not to speculate too much.

Nearly two months passed. Brad recovered rapidly from his physical injuries and even made friends with Sheriff Nick Scarpelli, swapping war stories about being cops in the urban trenches. He still suffered from selective amnesia, though, and did not recall all of his initial experiences with Jeremy.

Rob, the college student Jeremy had shared with Samantha in the hotel in New Orleans, became a frequent visitor, completing his graduate studies in Colorado and his sex education at Jeremy's ranch in Wyoming, where he found no shortage of willing tutors.

The second week of November, Jeremy said to Brandon and Brad, "Let's go for a ride."
"OK, where are we going?"
"You'll see."
They drove west on I-80 to 15th Street and then east on Willett Drive to the University of Wyoming Sports

Complex, where they watched the football team practice for that weekend's game with BYU.

"This is great!" said Brandon. "How did you know I was a big football fan?"

"I didn't, but I was hoping you were. Let's go say hello to the guys."

"Huh?" Brandon was amazed that they could get into the locker room with the players. As they were sashaying down the ramp into the locker room area, Brandon spotted several plaques bearing Jeremy's name and pictures of him in a University of Wyoming football uniform on the walls. "You played here?"

"I told you I had connections."

"Yeah, but—"

"Oh, my god!" exclaimed one of the players. "Isn't that Bullet Travis?"

Brandon could not decide which excited him more: the sight of all those gorgeous jocks, many of whom were now naked or close to it, or the fact that all of them seemed to know who Jeremy was.

"Listen up, guys," announced the coach. "I'm sure you all know Bullet Travis. Hell, you probably watched every game he played when you were kids. Well, he's asked to say a few words, and I didn't think anybody would mind. Hell, I sure don't. Bullet."

"Hi, guys. Who's gonna win the game this weekend?"

"Cowboys! Cowboys! Cowboys!" chanted the entire team.

"Good. That's what I wanna hear. I know you guys are gonna cream their asses, and I'm gonna have a little reward for you. I'm inviting all you guys to a little barbecue at my ranch with some of the best Angus beef you ever tasted. We'll have all the fixin's, plenty of liquid refreshments, and maybe a little entertainment. You can bring your dates too."

Cheers went up among the players, and Brandon smiled broadly at his buddy's generosity.

"There's one thing I want you guys to do for me, though...besides win the game, that is."

"Sure, Bullet," said the team captain. "Just name it. You know we'd do anything for you...even without the cookout."

"Thanks, Steve."

The captain beamed over the fact that Jeremy knew his name.

"I want you guys to meet a couple of people," said Jeremy. "This is my very good friend Brad," said Jeremy pulling Brad close to his body. "And this is my cousin Brandon." (Yes, he called Brandon his cousin even though the wedding had been called off, so they were not really family. Not that kind of family anyway, but family nonetheless.)

"Come January, Brandon's gonna be a student here at UW. Now, as you can see," he said, rubbing his hand over the young man's well-defined chest and arms, "Brandon's quite capable of taking care of himself, but you'll forgive me if I'm a little over-protective. So, I'm asking you men to look out for him. You'll also find that Brandon is very smart, and I'm sure he won't mind providing a little tutoring from time to time. Then again, probably none of you guys needs any tutoring, huh?"

That little tease nearly brought down the house as one player after another started poking the guy next to him and trading fraternal insults.

Steve, the team captain, stepped forward and shook Brandon's hand. "Whaddya say, sport? Wanna be an honorary UW Cowboy?" Brandon beamed.

"Jenkins!" barked the coach. "Go get your new teammate here a jersey—number 7."

"Right away, Coach."

"Number 7?" Brandon asked. "Isn't that the number Jeremy wore when he played here? I saw the photos on the wall."

"That's right, kid." And Brandon nearly burst with pride, though he tried in vain to conceal it as much as he could.

"One thing, Coach. Why do all you guys call him Bullet?"

Putting his hand on Brandon's shoulder, the coach answered, "Because when he played quarterback here, nobody could run faster or throw the ball farther than Jeremy Travis. He still holds several school records. That's what those plaques are for. Bullet Travis is a legend on this campus. Trust me, son, these guys would do anything for him, and ain't nobody gonna mess with Bullet Travis' cousin."

All the players crowded around Jeremy to ask for his autograph and hear stories about his days as the star quarterback and around Brandon to welcome him to the team. For the second time in his life, Brandon Miller had been adopted.

On their way out of the locker room, they were pulled aside by Steve, the team captain. "Bullet...uh, Mr. Travis—"

"You can call me Bullet or Jeremy," interrupted Number 7. "Whatever makes you more comfortable."

"Thanks, Jeremy. Uh, you said we could bring a date to the party at your place."

"Of course!"

"Well, you won't mind if I bring my boyfriend, will you?"

Jeremy smiled. "Of course not, I'm looking forward to meeting him."

"You already have, sir...uh, Jeremy...you just didn't know it." He nodded in the direction of Jenkins, the team manager who had brought Brandon his jersey. Looking more closely now, Jeremy could see it in the way they looked at each other. "We haven't told the guys, but I think now maybe it's time." Jeremy shook his hand and congratulated him.

Walking back out of the locker room, Brad stopped to study one of the photographs. It showed Bullet Travis diving over a mountain of football players converging in a goal-line stand. Finally, after a long period of intense concentration, Brad said, "Superman." Then, he turned to Jeremy and poked him in the ribs, "Superman!"

Stunned, Jeremy asked Brad, "Do you remember that night on Burgundy Street as we were walking to your apartment?"

"Yes, Jack. I remember. I remember."

"Jack? You called me Jack?"

"Would you rather I called you Jeremy?"

"Oh, baby, you can call me anything you like." And with that, Jeremy and Brad fell into a deep, long kiss.

As they had promised the Millers, Jeremy, Ford, and Brandon spent Thanksgiving at their farm in Texas. Though it had been a trying year, all of them felt that they had much to be thankful for. Brandon practically gushed over his new friendships with the cowboys on the ranch— especially Randy—and the Cowboys at the university, who had even promised to take him with them if—no, *when*— they made it to a bowl game. "Cowboys! Cowboys! Cowboys!" Seth Miller glowed in the opportunity to talk football with his son and Jeremy. Carol Miller couldn't care less about football, but she delighted in seeing her family so happy.

For Christmas, the Millers joined the Leveques, including Amy at the Travis' ranch. "You could have brought Paul," Jeremy said to Amy. "It would have been OK."

"Well, about that," Amy replied, "we broke up." Seeing the shock on Jeremy's face, she continued, "Like you, Jeremy, we have moved on. None of us is the same person we were just a short time ago. Don't get me wrong," she hastened to add, "I still love him...just as I still love you...but it's a different kind of love now."

"So, what now?" Jeremy asked.

"I believe Mr. Right is still out there, but until he shows up, I'm going to focus on helping other people. Dad has decided to set up a foundation to support gay youths, and he has asked me to run it."

"That's fantastic," exclaimed Jeremy, giving her a great big hug.

After opening their presents Christmas morning, Brad stood in front of the crackling fireplace and requested everyone's attention.

"Mother, Dad, Uncle Seth, Aunt Carol...Jeremy and I have something to tell you."

"Must be serious," said Mr. Leveque. "What is it, Son?"

"Jeremy...Jeremy has asked me to marry him. Of course, we can't legally get married in Wyoming," he added hastily, "but Wade Dawkins has agreed to perform a commitment ceremony, and we'd like you to be here." The sudden silence concerned both Jeremy and Brad. "Mama? Dad?"

"I'm sorry, Ford," Marie Leveque finally responded. "This is just not the future I had always envisioned for my son, but if this is what you want, of course we'll be here. Wild horses couldn't keep us away!"

"Oh, Mama. Thank you. Thank you. I love you so much." Tears formed in Brad's eyes as he hugged his mother tightly.

"Welcome to the family, Son," said Mr. Leveque to Jeremy. *Son.* No one had called him that since his parents died. He liked the sound of it.

Marie Leveque broke Ford's embrace and hugged Jeremy. Then, she kissed Jeremy on both cheeks and then lightly on the lips. "Oooh! Nice kisser!" she teased Ford. "I can see why you're so fond of him."

"Maaamaaa!"

Also by Brock Archer

Brock Archer's MEN (2022). Phoenix: Brock Archer Arts. www.brockarcher.net.

About Brock Archer

Brock Archer has been writing homoerotic fiction for nearly two decades, but his writings have been posted mostly online, where they have received rave reviews and very high ratings from readers. *Discoveries* is his first novel to appear in print and e-book.

In addition to being an accomplished writer of gay fiction, he is also a published poet and a songwriter.

He is also an internationally recognized digital artist. His artwork has been featured in art shows in New York, California, Arizona, and Germany and online. His work has appeared in books, journals, and magazines in the United States, Germany, and Ukraine as well as his own artbook, *Brock Archer's MEN*.

Brock can be reached through his website: www.brockarcher.net.